Morgan Library Ghost Stories

MORGAN LIBRARY GHOST STORIES

EDITED BY

Inge Dupont and Hope Mayo

WITH AN INTRODUCTION BY

Hope Mayo

WOOD ENGRAVINGS BY

John De Pol

FORDHAM UNIVERSITY PRESS

NEW YORK • MCMXC

CONTENTS

List of Illustrations

INTRODUCTION

HOPE MAYO

This volume of *Morgan Library Ghost Stories* had its origin in an exhibition entitled "Pierpont Morgan's Manuscripts and M. R. James," sponsored by the Library in the spring of 1987 as a part of the 150th anniversary celebration of Pierpont Morgan's birth. In a lecture with the same title as the exhibition, given at the Library on 27 May 1987, I explored in some detail the work done by Montague Rhodes James, the foremost medieval manuscript scholar of his day, on the first, and still the only, published catalogue of Morgan Library manuscripts. Important as James's work on this and other catalogues was in developing techniques for the study of the medieval book, he is known far more widely as the author of *Ghost Stories of an Antiquary* and several similar collections. Even people who are completely unaware of his scholarly attainments and know nothing of the subjects of his erudition appreciate the manner in which he used his knowledge of medieval artifacts and scholarly settings to create a convincing atmosphere for some of the best stories of the supernatural ever written in English. Scholars also respond to his sureness of touch in this regard, and in the course of my lecture I pointed out that this aspect of his career involved James in hitherto unknown contact with the Morgan Library, in that

Belle da Costa Greene, the Library's first director, not only consulted him about manuscripts in the collection but implored him to write a ghost story for her. A few paragraphs of explanation based on the lecture will provide historical background both for the individual stories presented in this collection and for the circumstances of their creation.

Pierpont Morgan began seriously collecting books and art only after the death of his father in 1890, at which time he himself was more than fifty years old. Junius Morgan had himself been a collector, who owned, among other things, the manuscript of Sir Walter Scott's novel *Guy Mannering;* Pierpont Morgan later told his daughter Louisa that his own library had its beginning in his father's gift to him of this Scott manuscript. During the two decades after 1890 Pierpont Morgan acquired additional historical and literary autographs, including manuscripts of nine more of Scott's Waverley novels and *The Lady of the Lake.* He also began collections of rare printed books and medieval illuminated manuscripts, counting among his early acquisitions, in 1896, a Gutenberg Bible printed on vellum, and in 1899, the ninth-century Lindau Gospels, now M. 1, known especially for its medieval jeweled and metal-work covers.

The book and manuscript collection now associated with the Morgan Library began to take form with three major purchases in the years 1899–1902. The Toovey collection, acquired in 1899 from the son of the English bookseller James Toovey, brought " 'an extensive and extraordinary assemblage of the productions of the Aldine Press' and a large number of volumes in fine bindings." With the library of Theodore Irwin of Oswego, New York, in 1900, came four Caxtons, the Golden Gospels, a tenth-century manuscript written in gold ink on purple-painted vellum, and several hundred prints, including many Rembrandt etchings. The third large purchase was the collection of Richard Bennett, which included both medieval illuminated manuscripts and a considerable number of early printed books. Bennett, an English manufacturer about whom little is known, seems to have begun collecting books in the 1890s. In 1897 he purchased the library of William Morris, from which he subsequently (in December 1898) sold all but 31 manuscripts and 239 printed books. By 1900 Bennett was seeking to sell his entire collection, consisting of 559 printed books and 107 manuscripts, and in 1902 Pierpont Morgan purchased it. The books acquired by Morgan for £140,000 or £200,000—the details of the sale are not well documented—were especially notable as including thirty-two Caxtons. After this, until his death in 1913, Morgan continued to buy printed books and medieval manuscripts individually or in smaller numbers from collections such as that of Lord Ashburnham.

As Morgan acquired collections, both of books and of art objects, he had them described by the authorities of the day. Illustrated catalogues of his manuscripts and early printed books, of his paintings, jewels, miniatures, porcelains, and bronzes, were sumptuously printed in limited editions for private distribution. Such catalogues served to enhance both his own pleasure in his collections and his status as a collector. Although a catalogue of the Toovey collection of books had appeared anonymously in 1901, the first of the truly lavish catalogues was that commissioned for the Bennett collection of medieval manuscripts and early printed books. Bernard Quaritch, the London bookseller with whom Morgan often dealt for his English purchases, acted as the agent, and acknowledged experts were engaged to prepare the descriptions: for the manuscripts, M. R. James, and for the early printed books, Robert Proctor, Alfred W. Pollard, and E. Gordon Duff. Work on the catalogue was carried out in England during the years 1902–1907, for it was only subsequently that the books were shipped to New York. James worked in Cambridge, where the manuscripts were sent carton by carton to him, Proctor and Pollard in London, and Duff in Manchester. The four folio volumes which resulted, one for the medieval manuscripts, three for the early printed books, were printed by the Chiswick Press in 1906–1907, under the title *Catalogue of Manuscripts and Early Printed Books from the Libraries of William Morris, Richard Bennett, Bertram, Fourth Earl of Ashburnham and Other Sources, Now Forming Portion of the Library of J. Pierpont Morgan.*

In the years after the purchase of the Bennett collection in 1902, the primacy of Morgan's library among his collections became apparent. During this period he worked closely with Charles McKim, of the prominent architectural firm McKim, Mead and White, to plan and construct a special library building next to his home on East 36th

The Courtyard

Street in New York. And by the time the building was completed, he had hired a librarian to preside over the organization of his collections in it.

Belle da Costa Greene had gone to work as a young woman in the Princeton University Library, where she learned the rudiments of cataloguing and reference work and served a brief apprenticeship in rare books under Ernest Cushing Richardson, then professor of bibliography and university librarian. There her passion for early books and manuscripts attracted the attention of Junius Spencer Morgan at a time when his uncle, Pierpont Morgan, was looking for someone to take charge of his library. On Junius's advice, Miss Greene was given the post in 1905, when she was 21 years old.

From the first, she and Morgan got along well. He liked her quick mind and ready tongue, and she admired his decisiveness and magnificent style, so that loyalty and affection soon answered one another. She came to rely on Morgan as on a father, and his death in Rome in 1913 came as a great shock to her. In her sorrow, she wrote to a friend: "His never-failing sympathy, his understanding and his great confidence and trust in me, bridged all the difference in age, wealth and position."

Belle da Costa Greene was described as a short, slim-waisted, dark-haired, gray or green-eyed young woman. Vivacious and attractive, she did not hesitate to adopt the grand manner that she felt suited her role. Her energy and enthusiasm for her work were legendary, as was her talent for friendship that enabled her to maintain many close contacts even through long separations of time and distance. Hospitable and helpful to serious scholars, whether they were acknowledged experts or untried students, she was intolerant of mediocrity and commanded an imperiousness of manner which she did not hesitate to use against the pompous or the incompetent. "If a person is a worm," she is said to have remarked, "you step on him." While she could be frank and indiscreet, she was also skillful and uncompromising in defending the interests of the library to which she devoted her life with passionate interest.

After Pierpont Morgan's death, Miss Greene continued in her post as private librarian to J. P. Morgan, Jr., and when he provided for the establishment of the library as an independent institution in 1924, she was appointed by the Board of Trustees as its first director, a position in which she remained until her retirement in 1948.

Much of the work on the Bennett catalogue, in particular James's contribution to it, was done by the time Miss Greene went to work for Pierpont Morgan. In 1914–1915, however, shortly after Morgan's death, she corresponded with M. R. James regarding a manuscript of Beatus of Liébana's Commentary on the Apocalypse (now M.429) which she had bought a few years previously. In the 1920s James cooperated with Sydney Cockerell in editing the facsimile edition of M.638, *A Book of Old Testament Illustrations of the Middle of the Thirteenth Century Sent by Cardinal Bernard Maciejowski to Shah Abbas the Great, King of Persia, Now*

13

in the Pierpont Morgan Library at New York, which J. P. Morgan presented to the Roxburghe Club. When this was published in 1927, Miss Greene wrote to James, expressing her appreciation for his contribution to the introduction, which she claimed to be reading for the third time, as Mr. Morgan was for the second. In this letter of 22 April 1927 she continued:

I so much wish that we could induce you to come over here, as our guest, for a few months in either 1928 or 1929—to see and help us with some of our new manuscripts and perhaps give a series of informal talks to the group of us over here, who are working, as best we can without any leader, upon manuscripts—Is there the *slightest* possibility that you would consider this?

James replied, after thanking her for her comments on the book:

The splendid invitation you extend to me is another pleasure: but I don't believe I shall ever cross the water: I think I've put it off too long. And of course if I did come, and attempted to cross the street in New York, that would be the end of it all: at least, that is the impression I have formed....

This exchange initiated a correspondence between James in England and J. P. Morgan and Miss Greene in New York, lasting at least until 1933, in which Morgan repeatedly invited James to visit the Library and Miss Greene solicited notes about manuscripts. The two Americans, however, were also sensible to James's reputation in other areas, and Miss Greene wrote as early as 1927: "we both hope that in your busy life, you are finding time for another of our *favourite* ghost stories!" In 1933 she renewed her appeal: "Mr. Morgan and I have long been crying 'out of the depths' for a new ghost story from your hand.Won't you give us one soon?" To this James replied, in his last known letter to her: "I am afraid the vein of ghost stories has run rather dry. If it opens again, you shall know." Unfortunately, by 1933 the vein had run dry, and the Library has had to content itself with the manuscript of the late story "A Warning to the Curious," sold after James's death and presented as a gift by J. P. Morgan in 1942.

When, in May 1987, I ended my public lecture on M. R. James by regretting that he never visited New York and so was never inspired to write a Morgan Library ghost story, there were two consequences: Richard Priest, represented in this volume as the author of "Non Furtum Facies," wrote and pseudonymously circulated among the Morgan Library staff a bibliographical ghost story entitled "The Nagrom Library," and this prompted Inge Dupont to propose a ghost-story writing competition, for which the two conditions were that the stories be in the style of M. R. James and that they relate in some way to the Morgan Library. Francis S. Mason, then Acting Director of the Library, consented to sponsor the contest, and in the autumn of 1987, he, Charles E. Pierce, Jr., the newly appointed Director of the Library, and James H. Heineman, a long-time member of the Board of Trustees, reviewed the stories to select three for a public reading. This took place at the Library in December 1987, at which time Mr. Mason gave impressive renditions of "Non Furtum Facies," "The Clergyman's Bargain," and "The Ballad of the Belle." The seven stories published here represent a selection from those submitted to the contest, and the editors hope they will go some way toward filling the lacuna in the history of the Morgan Library created by M. R. James's failure to respond to Belle Greene's plea.

We are grateful to all who helped make the ghost story contest a success, to the authors who have contributed their work to this collection, to G. Thomas Tanselle for his suggestion that the stories be published, to John De Pol for his suitably atmospheric illustrations, and to Morris A. Gelfand for his enthusiastic sponsorship of this volume. We also wish to thank our colleagues Herbert Cahoon, Paul Needham, J. Rigbie Turner, William M. Voelkle, and David W. Wright for supplying information about the early history of Pierpont Morgan's collecting. The Pierpont Morgan Library gave permission to quote from the correspondence of Belle da Costa Greene, as well as from various publications issued by the Library, and N.J.R. James has graciously allowed us to quote from unpublished letters of M. R. James.

Morgan Library Ghost Stories

Old Macgregor: A Tale of Hallowe'en

Rhoda Mansbach

T WAS Hallowe'en. In appropri-
ate costume and mask, the staff of the Pontpierre Library
had performed the rites established by the Founder himself
in honor of the day. In that study from which he had gone
out to conquer fresh worlds and acquire yet another
sculptured Madonna, another jewel-encrusted missal, they
had bobbed for apples, played charades, and recited party
pieces under his stern, painted gaze. The director had read
from Mr. Montague James's *Ghost Stories*, the assistant
director had recited "Tam O'Shanter" (this in memory of
the Founder whose party piece it had been), the curator of
music manuscripts had given a rousing rendition of "The
Erl King." But now, at last, the claret, the brioche sand-
wiches, the neat stacks of petit-fours had all been cleared
away. Now the sputtering candles shed but a faint glow on

19

the red silk wall-covering with the Chigi emblem, and shadows shrouded the portraits of the Founder and his son. Against the stained-glass window-panes the dark night pressed its velvet back like a well-fed panther, while on the hearth the dying embers of the fire glowed feebly.

The room was empty save for the curator emeritus of autograph manuscripts who, overcome by wine and exertion, had fallen asleep in one of the red velvet arm chairs by the fireplace and been overlooked. In the logs' dim glow his cherubic face with its pink cheeks and still-smooth skin looked as placid as that of a contented infant. The last log fell, sending a shower of sparks up the chimney, and he woke with a start, still smiling, from a pleasant dream in which, browsing through a pile of books in an old book shop near the British Museum, he had stumbled across the autograph manuscript of Edward Fitzgerald's translation of the *Agamemnon*, believed to have been destroyed when the privately printed edition of the work appeared in 1865. For a moment he gazed around him, still groggy from sleep, unable to recognize his surroundings. Memory returned, and with it the realization he was not alone. Someone else was in the room, stumbling around in the dark. That someone cursed as he fell over a chair and stubbed his toe on the Founder's desk.

"Who's there?" asked the curator emeritus, startled.

"It's me, Stanley," came an irritated voice. "I'm trying to find an earring."

Ah, the new page in the Reading Room to whom he had

been introduced in the course of the evening's festivities. He had come to the party as a member of a rock group called The Unquiet Dead, his understanding of a costume appropriate to Hallowe'en. It had not been an inspired choice, the curator emeritus reflected. The black sleeveless T-shirt did nothing for his complexion or his physique, the tight black jeans merely emphasized his flabbiness, and the high-heeled black boots showed only he didn't do well in heels. (The curator emeritus took the privilege of age to attend the annual function in the neat three-piece pin-striped gray suit with black patent shoes which had been his uniform during his active years.)

"This dumb party," the young man went on, "dressing up and bobbing for apples and reading ghost stories. What a crock!"

"You don't like Hallowe'en?" observed the curator emeritus mildly. "I am surprised. It gives one an opportunity to forget the oppressive rationality of the everyday world and indulge one's atavistic superstitions, those childish fears about ghosts and the supernatural which the twentieth century tries so hard to repress."

"I don't believe in ghosts," snorted the young man who had by now given up his pursuit of the elusive earring and thrown himself moodily into the chair opposite. "They're dumb."

"Ah, a follower of Pyrrhon." The curator emeritus nodded understandingly. "Well, I suppose you are entitled to your opinion. As an old Latin professor of mine once

21

observed, on the subject of the pronunciation of the Latin *v* which I had been taught to render as a *w*, 'we may go on being wrong as long as we know we are wrong'."

The young man stared at him.

"What do you mean, 'wrong'? You don't really believe in ghosts, do you?"

"There are more things in heaven and earth, Horatio ..." replied the curator emeritus sententiously. "But let me tell you a story which happened here in this very library ..."

"I think I had better go," said the young man hastily, but the curator emeritus fixed him with an eye the Ancient Mariner might have envied, and he sank back sulkily into his chair.

"It happened some fifteen years ago," the curator emeritus began reminiscently, "when the melancholy task befell us of hiring a new page for the Reading Room. Old Vandercamp who had served us faithfully for sixty years—he had been hired by our first director herself—had at last become too old and infirm, too forgetful to stay with us any longer. His snoring too had begun to draw complaints from the readers. It wasn't easy to find a replacement. Such devoted loyalty, application, and exertion are not easy to come by in these materialistic times, particularly on the rather modest remuneration we offer. Several applicants had offered themselves, but none seemed suitable. Only one remained to be interviewed. As he was ushered into the Reading Room, we could not fail to notice his difference from the others. Not only was he wearing a dark suit with a sparkling white shirt and well-polished shoes, unlike the other candidates who had sported those casual outfits left over from the sixties in which jeans and chains feature prominently, but there was an old-world courtesy about him, and a fluent articulateness of speech, which were in marked contrast with the informal vernacular grunts to which the others had subjected us. Such an old-world air was indeed in no way surprising since he proved to come from Scotland. He introduced himself as 'Mr. Francis Osbaldistone Macgregor,' explaining, when we all questioned him about this singular praenomen, that his mother had been a great devotee of the Wizard of the North." Here the curator emeritus broke off. "You seem bemused, young man. Does the name Francis Osbaldistone mean nothing to you?"

"No," retorted the young man. "Should it? And this *wizard*," a noticeable sneer in his voice, "has he something to do with your ghost story?"

"We shall see," replied the curator emeritus enigmatically. "Where was I? Ah, yes—Mr. Macgregor said he was a widower who had come to make his home in New York with his only daughter who had married an American businessman. Not wishing to be a burden financially, or be underfoot all day, he had decided to apply for this job for which, being a well-educated man and a lover of books, he felt himself eminently qualified. As he spoke I was puzzled, for I fancied I had seen him somewhere before but I could not place him." The curator emeritus fetched out his pipe and eyed the young man who was fidgeting impatiently.

23

"I was right—as you shall shortly hear."

"Will it take long?" burst out the young man. "Besides, I still don't see what this has to do with ghosts."

"You will," replied the curator emeritus equably. "To resume. Mr. Macgregor was engaged. Indeed we all congratulated ourselves on finding such a treasure. He not only had that dignified manner of which I have spoken, but he proved himself well-informed about literature, particularly the works of the eighteenth century in England and Scotland. He was at home with Latin, French, and German; he could read Greek when necessary. In addition, he was a punctual and zealous worker, sometimes, indeed, a little too zealous. If a reader inadvertently turned the page of a rare book too hastily, Mr. Macgregor was upon him, reprimanding him loudly for his carelessness. Once, when a distinguished professor from Germany sneezed too close to an illuminated page, he came running forward with a large handkerchief. If a reader requested several books or manuscripts, Mr. Macgregor would issue them according to the timetable *he* expected him to follow, rather than that of the reader himself. He would even set a reader right on matters of scholarship when they touched upon the works of his favorite, the creator of his eponymous ancestor. But these little foibles, signs of commitment to the task in hand, could easily be forgiven. Meanwhile he and I discovered a shared interest in opera. One night, by chance, we found ourselves sitting beside each other at the Met. It was that famous occasion," the curator emeritus closed his eyes dreamily,

The West Room

"in which Joan Sutherland made her trans-Atlantic debut in *Lucia*. Mr. Macgregor was much taken with the music and the singing but displayed great agitation at the libretto. Where had thon Italian, he wanted to know, got his notions o' Scottish history? It wasna frae *The Bride o' Lammermoor*. But what is wrong, young man?" the curator emeritus broke off. "You appear restless."

"Will you get to the *point*?" choked the young man. "I thought you were telling a ghost story."

"And so I am. As I said, we found Mr. Macgregor an asset, and things went on smoothly, until, that is, the day that Dr. James Mackintosh, one of Britain's prominent Scott scholars, asked to see me on a matter of great urgency and confidentiality. It took him some time to get to the point—which was that he suspected grave misdemeanor on the part of the library. Collating the manuscript of *Old Mortality* with the first edition in preparation for a new definitive edition, he had come across corrections not reported by any previous scholar. Scott, as is well known, wrote in a large quarto notebook with two leaves open side-by-side. He wrote very fluently in a dense, close script on the recto side of a leaf, and, since there was no room for alterations within the lines, used the blank page of the verso facing it for corrections and afterthoughts of which there was often a considerable number. It was to some of these that Dr. Mackintosh now drew my attention. The penmanship matched that of the original but the ink was recent. Clearly someone had inserted well-forged corrections into the text. Yet this seemed impossible. Our strict rules governing the use of pencil, the reputation of the scholars to whom such a manuscript would be issued, the vigilance of the Reading Room staff—all these seemed to preclude such a thing. Besides, what purpose, I asked, could there be to such a forgery? An observation, I may add, of a remarkable naiveté, as Dr. Macintosh was quick to point out. The establishment of one's reputation by the discovery of hitherto-unknown readings was more than sufficient inducement for a young and aspiring scholar, especially one on whom the grace of tenure had not yet been bestowed. He had come to me, Dr. Mackintosh then went on, before deciding what to do. If it were to become known that manuscripts in the Pontpierre Library were being tampered with—if not by a reader, then by a staff member...."

His words, the curator emeritus was glad to see, had at last made an impression on his listener. Even in the dim firelight, he looked visibly shaken.

"You mean some one had written on an original manuscript worth thousands of dollars?" he whispered in awe-struck tones. "That's obscene."

The curator emeritus nodded approvingly. The basic sentiment was appropriate although he himself would have expressed it in less mercenary terms. (The curator emeritus eschewed vulgarity.) He resumed his tale.

"Of course, I then asked Dr. Mackintosh to show me the manuscript in question," he went on, "and we set about immediately checking the remaining Scott manuscripts,

27

working after hours together in the Reading Room on the pretext of a press deadline. After two days we had carefully checked everything. The library has eight novels entire, parts only of *Ivanhoe* and *Waverley*. The same thing in all, the poems had not been touched—as yet. Dr. Mackintosh was then forced to leave for a seminar at Harvard, and the following night I embarked alone on the next task—endeavoring to trace a pattern in the corrections and emendations, and at the same time to check the files indicating to whom the manuscripts had been issued in the past few years."

Here the curator emeritus paused and, fixing his young companion with a stern stare, observed parenthetically: "That is the reason, my dear boy, for our preternatural fussiness over entries into the log-book which people have been heard to grumble about." He continued. "It was then I noticed an odd circumstance. Whoever had made the emendations seemed to have been possessed of a literary bent. In almost every case the corrections and additions improved the original. We were not dealing with some hack of a graduate student, but with a fine literary mind which knew its author well. With this clue, I searched the files to see who, of reputation, had requested any of the manuscripts in the last few years. Only a few names turned up, but they were of scholars of such eminence, I hesitated how to approach them. Moreover, the greater number of people who knew about our little problem, the greater the likelihood that some rumor would leak out, destructive to the reputation of the Library.

"As I sat there lost in thought, not knowing what to do for the best, I became aware of movement elsewhere in the library. I stiffened and turned—to see Mr. Macgregor sitting at his desk. I had not heard him come in, and he was at first equally oblivious to my presence. He seemed to me from where I sat to be writing busily, but when I moved and thus alerted him,

" 'Who's there?' he said. 'Is that yourself, Mr. Colquohoun?'

"I said that it was and expressed myself surprised that he should have been working at such a late hour. At the same time a horrid and monstrous suspicion entered my mind.

"Mr. Macgregor said he often worked late, tidying up, dusting, reshelving books, and I now remembered that I had seen him at work after-hours on several occasions. I then asked him to help me reshelve the books I had been working on, which he did, with only a cursory glance at them, showing no particular interest. Nor was there any 'starting like a guilty thing surprised.' I managed to contrive it that he and I left at the same time, and I determined to voice my suspicions to the director first thing in the morning. You can imagine my dismay when, the next day, there was no sign of Mr. Macgregor. Nor could any trace of him be found. Phone calls to the number he had given us met with the recorded message that there was no such number. An expedition undertaken by myself and one of the guards to the supposed address showed it to be non-existent. Frantic, I rushed to check the manuscripts again. I had counted eight and two thirds and was congratulating myself on my acumen of the previous evening in cajoling Mr. Macgregor into leaving with me, when, to my horror, on opening the case that contained *Waverley*, I discovered it—empty! Empty, that is, except for a letter in my own writing to the curator of the National Library of Scotland, regretfully refusing his request that the Pontpierre Library lend him our portion of the manuscript of *Waverley* for its exhibition in honor of the bicentenary of Sir Walter Scott's birth, and a thick piece of quarto. This, when shaken, fell neatly open to reveal two leaves on which was written, in a hand not unknown to me, a short story entitled 'Wandering Wallie's Tale.' At that moment I realized why Mr. Macgregor had seemed so familiar. Not long before, I had had occasion to show to one of our readers Bulwer-Lytton's article, 'Death of Sir Walter Scott,' which he wrote in 1832 for *New Monthly Magazine*. Inserted in the slim pamphlet is an original pen-and-ink portrait of the master himself, with the note, 'Done from recollection, June, 1836, by J-----------'."

The curator emeritus paused dramatically to allow the implication of his words to sink in, but all the young man said, in disappointed tone, was:

"So it was Macgregor. Big deal. You said it was a *ghost* story. Did you get the manuscript back?"

"I haven't finished," the curator emeritus said patiently. "The next morning a long-distance call from the curator of the National Library of Scotland thanked me for our generous donation of fifteen leaves of the manuscript of *Waverley* which had taken him completely by surprise. He could only conjecture, he said in a dry tone, that some guardian angel had heard his prayers and inspired us to exchange our refusal of a loan to an outright gift.

"As I was still reeling from this blow, Dr. Mackintosh, who had returned from Harvard in response to our hasty summons, verified the script, the language, and the style of the story as an authentic hitherto-unknown work by Sir Walter Scott. A tale of the supernatural, like 'Wandering Willie's Tale' in *Redgauntlet*, it recounted, he said, the story of a 'makar' who had made his native land legendary in story and verse but whose manuscripts now lay scattered, far from their native soil. One day as this 'makar' is singing Hosannas in the heavenly choir, he is summoned to the presence of the Almighty who tells him that he has decided to hearken to a wee prayer put up by a worthy and respectable gentleman, a pillar o' the Kirk, and send him back to earth for a few weeks to retrieve a part of one of his manuscripts from the hands of the Philistines who have despoiled his heritage.

"Here Dr. Mackintosh paused and looked at me, frowning.

" 'This tale is clearly an allegory,' he said, 'but it will take some time to decipher it. During his lifetime Scott was pragmatic about his work, yet this story suggests a deep concern about the fate of his manuscripts after his death. It is a new angle I shall have to investigate. Indeed, what with this discovery, and the alterations in the other manuscripts,

I don't quite know what to think. Yet I cannot believe that they are forgeries....'

"He paused expectantly, but I said nothing to enlighten him although the explanation of the emendations in the other manuscripts was now also clear to me—an effort on the part of Mr. Macgregor to improve the shining hour, so to speak. Instead I contrived to indicate quietly to Dr. Mackintosh that in return for his discretion in the matter of this unexpected discovery and the peculiar circumstances attending it, he might have exclusive access to the manuscripts—a suggestion in which, after a moment's hesitation, he was only too pleased to acquiesce."

The curator emeritus ceased. At last, he saw, his words had had their effect. In the dying light of the last, flickering candle, the young man's face grew pale. His eyes widened. A sadder and wiser lad he rose to his feet and tottered from the room as the clock in the corner chimed midnight. Hallowe'en was over for another year.

Lily Hodge
Herbert Cahoon

N THE EVENTFUL YEARS of my curatorship I have had the opportunity of acquiring many literary and historical letters and manuscripts for my library, an institution internationally known for its services to scholarship. This, currently and in retrospect, gives me much pleasure. The letters and manuscripts come to us in various ways, as appropriate and welcome gifts, in more or less routine purchases, from auction rooms where bidding is usually touched with some degree of excitement, and in private transactions. This last method of acquisition can be satisfying to all parties, but it generally requires a considerable expenditure of time and sometimes involves visits to private collections. A few years ago, after a series of inconclusive negotiations about inherited collections and family papers, I began to chafe at this type of appointment and the uncertainties that seemed increasingly to attend it.

My first meeting with Lily Hodge, however, produced in my psyche (I do not know how else to describe it) quite a different reaction, and a positive zest for acquisition. She had made an appointment by telephone, spoke of an important gift, and appeared in my office late in the morning of September eighteenth. Her appearance took me quite by surprise, and I was instantly captivated: jet black hair and eyes a fascinating yellow-green. Gold bracelets and a gold chain were the only ornaments for her stylish black dress. She was extremely graceful, and her slender body had, I thought, a true feline elegance.

She sat down in the visitor's chair and came directly to the point. "Would you like to have the Samuel Johnson–James Boswell correspondence—both sides?" she asked.

I was stunned and speechless yet managed to mumble, "But it is certainly lost."

"Certainly not."

"But—"

She clearly relished my surprise and consternation; her mouth almost formed a smile. I composed myself as best I could and, with gentle, soothing questions, asked for more information. I also desperately tried to recall what David Buchanan had written about these lost letters.

"They are safe in New York and I can bring them here."

"Are you empowered to act for the owner?"

"I am the owner," she replied.

"I would very much like to see them, and I thank you for coming to the library." My remark was unequal to the occasion, but my mind was whirling at the thought of holding in my hands those precious letters. If Lily Hodge were speaking the truth, this would be one of the greatest discoveries in the history of English Literature, and scholarship was ripe to receive it. What would the price be, and who could afford them?

"You will hear from me again, I promise. I am offering them to no one else, and you must not speak of them to anyone. You may be interested to know that I have a considerable knowledge of many academic institutions, and have experience in scholarly research. Before I leave I am going to give you a copy of a recent article." She rose and took a slender offprint from her handbag, as I escorted her to the door. It was "The Cat's Purr as Defense Mechanism," by Lily Hodge, reprinted from an annual volume of *Acta Felisologia,* a publication of which I had never heard.

"There are well over two hundred letters here," she said, "more from Boswell to Johnson than on the other side. I am the owner and the emissary."

Lily Hodge had brought packets of letters, tied with faded ribbons inside torn heavy wrappers that had once been sealed, in a modern carrying case; she was most punctual in this new appointment made for late in the afternoon of the eighteenth of October. She had kept me on tenterhooks for a month, and I had, of course, not dared to breathe a word of the letters to anyone, not even in the interests of fund raising.

I examined a few of the letters from each correspondent

35

and was nearly numb with excitement. The letters were perfectly preserved, and as I unfolded and read them, I recognized passages that Boswell had used in his *Life of Samuel Johnson LL.D.*, published in 1791, for I had returned to the great biography and spent many hours with it.

I looked at Lily Hodge and took a deep breath. "I must ask the price."

"They are yours as a gift," she answered.

I started to express my profound thanks, but she continued.

"I admire your library and believe that it is an appropriate home for these letters. I revere the memory of Dr. Johnson. Although I can do nothing to add to his reputation, I can supply information about him that the world will cherish. Dr. Johnson was a religious man who feared death and did not believe in a supernatural intelligence. But there were and are things he could not know. He loved and cared for his feline friends, a quality that has especially endeared him to me and, in a way, has brought us together beyond our times.

"You have an extraordinary interest in Dr. Johnson's cats," I said. I was in a maelstrom of confusion, ameliorated only by thoughts of our new acquisition, which I now accepted but still could not believe was real.

"As for Boswell," she added, "I loathe him and his memory, mainly because of his contempt for persons and situations he felt beneath him, especially cats. But the larger portion of the correspondence is from him, and he is a vital part of the picture. I made my first visit to you on Dr. Johnson's birthday as I believe in good auspices. You have a strong vault here in the library, I am sure."

I told her that I would let her accompany me (an unusual procedure) to place the letters in our vault, where they would be protected by our security. Lily Hodge was pleased, and took—even stroked—my hand and made a grateful noise.

"In eternity," she said, "I believe Dr. Johnson has changed his ideas about America; he now finds it worthy of his interest and association. Therefore the letters are here. Boswell read little and thought little about America, but he now chortles with joy as American scholars continue to unveil his unacademic excesses."

As we descended to the basement, Lily Hodge revealed that she had obtained the letters from the vaults of Coutts' bank in London with the aid of a friendly spirit. "A friendly and resourceful spirit, I should say, for the bank never knew that they had them."

We placed the letters, unlabeled, in a recess of the vault befitting their importance. One of the great joys of my life has been to be orderly, as well as informal and inconsistent. I would willingly have passed the night with the letters, but that was not possible.

We made our way back to my office for the necessary paper work and a signed agreement, but when I stepped ahead to open a door and turned back to my guest and benefactor, she was not there. Lily Hodge had disappeared. To add to the mystery, I did not even have her address or telephone number. No guard had seen her leave the library. I was much upset by this combination of carelessness on my part and mystery on hers.

I made an appointment with the Director the following morning, and he agreed to come to the vault without knowing why. I fumbled with the combination lock, as usual, but managed to open the door without calling for assistance. I would let the Director open one of the packets of letters, for I knew he could easily recognize both handwritings. His joy, like mine, would know no bounds.

I led him to the recessed shelf and stopped just before I began to make an elegant gesture of presentation. The letters were not there.

"There were Johnson—Boswell letters here," I stammered, "and they are gone. I placed them on this shelf yesterday afternoon. What has happened to them?"

The Director generously tried to make sense out of my panic and confusion and somehow knew that my explanation might be a long one. There was no reason to remain in the vault for the letters simply were not there—anywhere. I notified security.

In my office I gave an oral report to the Director and promised to write a formal one. He left, and I began to compose myself and look for an explanation of the events that had brought and taken away a most precious literary heritage. I could find none, and had a melancholy feeling that I would never see the letters again. I felt I had been abandoned by reality, and I let my imagination dwell on wandering spirits and the supernatural. It was then that I heard the sad cries of a cat, slowly repeated; Lily Hodge, who had rarely left my thoughts, was, I somehow knew, sending me a message of frustration and defeat.

I reflected once more on Dr. Johnson and his immortal memory, and on James Boswell and his current and probably lasting fame. Only then did it come to me that yesterday had been the birthday of Boswell, the ailurophobic biographer. In the matter of the gift of letters to my library, his spirit had clearly been displeased and dominant.

Lex Talionis
J. Rigbie Turner

HE MOON ROSE SLOWLY over
the water like a great pellucid pearl set against the clear
cobalt sky. Its pale fire danced off water rippled by the sea-
breeze. Just above the water's surface two gulls glided in
unison as though moved by an unseen hand, their snow-
white wingtips almost touching. But as they approached
land, one veered back toward open water, while the other
floated on, without apparent exertion, over the broad sweep
of lawn bordering the bay, circled twice, dropped languidly
toward the ground, and at last came to rest, somewhat
unsteadily, on a jagged outcropping of rock some yards
from the water. The gull's head bobbed twice, turning
slightly each time, and it seemed to be listening to the
sounds of the party that floated across the lawn from the

veranda of the large house standing several hundred feet inland.

It was April 14th, 1987, and it was on that night that I met the ghost of Richard Strauss.

I had attended a party at the stately North Shore mansion belonging to my uncle and aunt, Rhode and Sheidora Aspinta, and, having tired of the noise and urgent conviviality of the festivities, had wandered away across the broad lawn to seek respite by the cool water's edge, where I had been standing for some time gazing out over the bay.

"How beautiful the *Princess Melosa* is tonight!"

I had been idly watching the gull, and turned abruptly to look at the man who had spoken. He was standing some yards away, also looking out over the bay.

"Pardon?"

"I was just admiring the yacht out in the harbor," the man said in a deep voice, his glottal *r*'s and smooth consonants suggesting European roots. "She is especially lovely just now, in the moonlight; she seems to glow, like an alabaster sculpture illuminated from within."

"She belongs to Rhode Aspinta, my uncle," I said.

"I know," the man said softly, the tone of his voice betraying the hint of a smile.

I looked back at him. He was tall, no longer young but with still finely etched features; what remained of his thinning hair lay in unruly wisps about his head, at times teased by vagrant breezes into a silver nimbus. I was sure I did not know him, had never met him before that moment, and was just as sure that he was not from the neighborhood. Yet although we had exchanged few words, and had only seen one another in the moonlight, something about his manner disturbed me.

"Are you a friend of the Aspintas?" I asked, more out of courtesy than from any wish to prolong our conversation.

"I have not actually met them," said the man softly. "But of course one hears much about a man of his reputation and power, and I have over the years made it a point to learn a good deal more."

Once again, an odd familiarity in the man's voice made me uneasy. The Aspintas were known throughout the country—and in fact far beyond—for their wealth, the opulence of the baronial house in front of which the stranger and I were now standing, the glittering parties such as the one I had just left, and the considerable influence my uncle wielded in local and state political affairs. I had in fact grown up not half a mile from the splendid mansion.

"Were you at the Aspintas' party?" I asked, knowing quite well that he had not been. "If so, I don't believe we were introduced, and if we were, I'm sorry to say I've quite forgotten it."

"No, Mr. Thobarran, I was not among the guests," said the man, smiling and extending a hand. "I am Bouquet, Richard Bouquet—an all too transparent *nom de guerre*, I admit, but one that a surprising number of people fail to recognize."

I was, admittedly, perplexed, but more by the fact that

the stranger knew my name than by the enigmatic nature of his introduction. Again the accent puzzled me: the softly guttural *r* followed by a gentle susurration in the first name suggested French origins, but the clipped consonants and smooth vowels in the last were faintly Germanic. But I felt somewhat more at ease, though whether from the fact that I now had a name to go with the shadowy figure or merely from the apparent grace of his manner, I was not sure.

"Mr. Bouquet, I gather, from the few words we've exchanged, that you know something about me, and I am, shall we say, puzzled, since so far as I know you are a stranger both to me and to my uncle and aunt. I hope you will not consider it an impertinence if I ask what, if any, your interest is in the *Melosa.*"

There was a pause of some moments before Bouquet answered; and when he did speak his voice was firm and calm, and his words were carefully chosen, as though he had long rehearsed what he had to say.

"I shall be happy to tell you why I am here, Mr. Thobarran. It is not a long story, but it *is* one of great import to us both. No, I should say that it is of considerable interest to me and that I do not believe you will find it of less than great concern to yourself.

"But first, since you clearly do not know who I am I suppose I should identify myself properly. In life, I was Richard Strauss, a composer of some renown, of whom you have perhaps heard. I died in 1949 and soon took the alternate name of Bouquet—a simple-minded transformation,

43

I admit, but one that allows me a degree of anonymity my real name would not."

I at once felt faint, and for a moment could not breathe, as though a great weight were pressing on my chest. Bouquet—no, I suppose I must call him by his real name, though to this day I still can scarcely acknowledge that this was, in fact, Richard Strauss's ghost—took me gently by the arm and led me a dozen yards to a wooden bench not far from the rock on which the gull had recently come to rest. The light from the house no longer reached us, and only the moonlight, bright and clear, illuminated the scene. I could not at first look at the man next to me but kept my eyes on the dappled water, and especially on the *Melosa*. My unease was, I am sure, readily apparent, and I did not speak, fearing that a trembling voice might betray my anxiety.

After a few moments, Strauss turned to me and spoke.

"Here is the story I have to tell. Many years ago—it was 1907, to be precise—plans were made to perform my opera *Salome* at the Metropolitan Opera House. It had first been given in Dresden a year or so before—God, what a night *that* was!—and it subsequently played in Prague, Berlin, Turin, and elsewhere. In each city it shocked and delighted; many persons condemned it, some tried to ban it, but no one could ignore it, and my fame—a pardonable boast, I think?—was assured. And it earned me a great deal of money as well.

"But the story in New York was of another order altogether. The general manager of the Metropolitan Opera in 1907 was Heinrich Conried. He decided, not without good reason, that my by then notorious work would be the ideal opera to present at his annual benefit. But Conried made what turned out to be a crucial mistake: he scheduled the dress rehearsal on a Sunday morning, January 20th, just at the time when the devout were either at church, or had just come from it. Oh, my opera was performed, all right, two days later, on Tuesday the 22nd, and Conried felt sure that a long and profitable engagement lay ahead. But something happened that week, something so singular and bizarre that to this day people speak of it, when it is discussed at all, in puzzled and skeptical tones.

"First there were the reviews," Strauss went on. "One of the most influential critics of the day was H. E. Krehbiel, of the *New York Tribune*. He averred that Wilde's drama was abhorrent, bestial, repellent, and loathsome; and he said of the opera—here I quote his exact words—that a reviewer should be an embodied conscience stung into righteous fury by the moral stench exhaled by the decadent and pestiferous work." Strauss paused, and I finally glanced at him; he was smiling, and the light from the water sparkled in his eyes.

"But while Krehbiel's righteous fulminations no doubt helped condemn *Salome*, his was not, ultimately, the voice that silenced mine. You see, two days after that first performance, the directors of the Metropolitan Opera & Real Estate Company—they were the persons who actually owned

45

the House—sent a resolution to Conried, the gist of which was that they considered the performance of *Salome* 'objectionable and detrimental' to the best interests of the organization, and therefore protested against any repetition of the work.

"Now, you might ask who these persons were whose influence was so great that by a stroke of the pen they could simply prohibit an opera they found distasteful. The *New York Tribune* reported that the objections started in the family of one of the most influential and powerful of the boxholders. It was, in fact, none other than *J. Pierpont Morgan.*" He spoke the name in slow, measured tones, pausing slightly between words. The effect, as I am sure he anticipated it would be, was immediate.

"Morgan!" I exclaimed. "But how could that be? It is well known that the man exercised enormous influence in the worlds of finance and business and that his rapacious collecting occasionally provoked both anxiety and awe among collectors and dealers. But opera! Did he truly have such power?"

"Obviously he did," Strauss said, and for the first time a hint of anger entered his voice. "But let me go on. Conried was a determined man and would not at first accept the decision. He petitioned to have the work restricted to non-subscription performances—that way, I suppose, people could have chosen whether or not they wished to submit themselves to this so-called 'objectionable and detrimental work' and would not be bound to it by a season subscription. But he was turned down. Then Conried threatened to put *Salome* on in another theatre, but his own directors thought that unwise. Finally, he capitulated, and dropped *Salome* from the repertory altogether. Morgan personally offered to reimburse Conried and his group, but they declined with thanks, preferring the record to show that the rebarbative work had been banned at their expense.

"That much, I think, is well known. But what has not been told is what happened subsequently, and"—here Bouquet paused and looked directly at me—"I think you will find it of exceptional interest. Or perhaps you know the next part of the story already?"

"No," I said, my voice low and slightly hoarse, "no, I'm largely ignorant of all this. Oh yes, I knew that something unpleasant had occurred around that time, that some scandalous opera had been closed, that a few prominent and wealthy individuals were involved, but it really was just so much gossip, and it all happened so long ago. Look," I said, getting up from the bench, "it's gotten quite late and I think I should go back to the party; I'm very tired and would most like to make my excuses and go home."

"Mr. Thobarren," said Strauss, now raising his voice. "I would ask that you stay; the rest of the story will not take long, and I can assure you that the dénouement will be, shall we say, dramatic."

I slowly sat down, my body slightly slouched, my eyes once more fixed on the *Melosa*.

"You see," Strauss continued, "Morgan's interest in

Salome did not end with the banning of the opera. Morgan, as I'm sure you know, had by that time been collecting for many years: rare books and manuscripts, paintings and drawings, tapestries, bronzes, glass, jewelry, furniture, sculpture—thousands upon thousands of treasures from all over Europe. And to house the books and manuscripts he had built one of the most splendid libraries in the country. Perhaps you have been there?"

"Of course," I answered, somewhat impatiently, "many times. In fact, my family and the Morgans were once quite close. My grandfather was a casual acquaintance of Pierpont Morgan, I think, and my uncle knew Pierpont Jr.; in fact, there were a number of Morgans—grandchildren and great-grandchildren I suppose they must be—at the Aspintas' party."

"You see," Strauss went on, "Morgan had outstanding collections of literary and historical manuscripts, but had never evinced any notable interest in music. In 1907 he had bought a very fine Beethoven manuscript in Florence, and he acquired some others over the years, as well as several hundred letters of composers, but toward the end of his life he was determined to make one truly memorable music acquisition, something that he could place with pride among his other great manuscripts. Of course, it could not be a major work by a minor composer, or a lesser work of an important one: he would only settle for a recognized masterpiece by a composer of international repute.

"In early April, 1912, I was at home in my villa in Garmisch, putting the final touches on my new opera, *Ariadne auf Naxos.* I received a letter from a Mr. Wheeler, at J. Pearson & Co., the antiquarian dealer in London. It seems that he had just gotten a letter from Belle da Costa Greene, Mr. Morgan's librarian, asking if Pearson could make enquiries —with the utmost discretion—to ascertain if by any chance the manuscript of *Salome* was available for sale to Mr. Morgan."

"Good Lord!" I exclaimed, now once more caught up in Strauss's story. "What an extraordinary turn of events! First, Morgan contemns the opera as morally reprehensible, secures a ban on it at the Metropolitan, causes you considerable financial loss—and five years later has the audacity to ask to buy the manuscript. How, when he got the manuscript, could he ever have explained the paradox of having sought out that which he once vilified?"

"Of course, I wondered the same thing myself," Strauss said with a chuckle. "And after some reflection I could find only one answer that made any sense to me. You see, though many accused him of unscrupulous practices in his collecting, and held him responsible for some singularly venal business activities, Morgan was a man of high character and was not, as some said at the time, without conscience. I came to the conclusion that he wished to accomplish two things: first, he wanted to add one major contemporary music manuscript to his collection; and second, he felt he should in some way repay me for the losses I had suffered in New York in 1907. He could not, five years later, simply send me money; that would have been out of the question. But by offering to buy the manuscript of the very work he had once scorned, he could at the same time assuage his conscience over my financial deprivations and add to his collection a work that would be worthy of it."

"Extraordinary!" I said, admitting to myself that his reasoning did make a good deal of sense. "But how would Morgan, having thus justified the purchase to himself, explain it to visitors to the Library who might remember the Conried episode? Surely some of *them* would rumor it about that Morgan's hypocrisy indeed knew no bounds."

"Yes, that occurred to me as well, and I concluded that one reason for the secrecy of Morgan's purchase was that, while Morgan wanted the manuscript for his archive, he never intended to show it to anyone. It would become part of that *sanctum sanctorum* which was said to be hidden away in the innermost depths of that magnificent Library, books and manuscripts that only he—and of course the impeccably discreet Miss Greene—knew of. The purchase would be our secret."

"Why did he consign the transaction to the Pearson firm?" I asked.

"That I do not know. Obviously he trusted them, had probably done considerable business with them before, and I can only surmise that he had the greatest respect for their probity. At any rate, Morgan made an extraordinarily generous offer: I shall not disclose the price he would pay for the manuscript; suffice it to say that it would have more than compensated me for my losses and that after only a few days' reflection I decided to accept the proposal. I sent the manuscript to London by special courier on the 4th of April. I got a cable from Wheeler two days later, announcing its safe arrival in Pall Mall Place, and on April 9th I received a letter saying that the manuscript would be sent to Morgan the next day."

"I assume Mr. Morgan paid promptly," I said, feeling some regret that this incredible story was nearly over. "But I am curious. Did you ever hear more from him about the matter? I should suppose not. Now that the circle was closed he surely had no reason to carry on any correspondence with you."

"No, I never heard from him again," Strauss replied, "but not for the reasons you might imagine. You see, he never got the manuscript of *Salome*."

"What?" I cried. "You mean Pearson never sent it?"

"Oh, it was sent; there is no question of that. But it never arrived in New York." He paused, and looked at me intently. "Does the date of April 14th, 1912, mean anything to you?"

For those of a certain age the date, exactly seventy-five years ago that night, was indelibly impressed on their memories. For others such as myself, of a younger generation, mention of it might not instantly recall its awful significance. But I knew it immediately, and the shock of recognition all but took my breath away.

"The *Titanic*!"

He nodded. We sat for some moments without speaking.

"Of course, my loss paled in significance to the appalling human tragedy of that dreadful night. But I would be less than honest if I did not admit to considerable regret that the manuscript was gone forever. Naturally, the opera had been printed years before, and neither my publisher nor I had any immediate need for the document. Still, it was like losing part of oneself; and Morgan *had* offered me a handsome payment for it...."

"Did you ever try to get in touch with him?"

"No. And, as I said, I never again heard from Morgan. But I learned years later—long after Morgan's death—that in his will Morgan had left your uncle's father a generous bequest, the amount of which was exactly equal to what Morgan had offered to pay me for the manuscript."

"But why? I know of course that he and Morgan were casual acquaintances and, I think, had some business dealings together. But still: I can think of no reason why Morgan should have left anything to my grandfather, let alone the amount he promised you—which must have been a considerable sum indeed."

"There is no reason why you should have known, Mr. Thobarren; it involves an episode about which neither your grandfather nor your uncle would have been likely to tell anyone, especially members of their family. In fact I only uncovered the full story quite recently. And *that* is why I am here tonight."

His voice, now tight and slightly menacing, made me

uneasy, and I shivered as a sudden breeze off the water chilled the air.

"You see, Morgan was one of the directors of the Metropolitan Opera & Real Estate Company, the very group that had expressed such displeasure in *Salome*. Your grandfather was also a director and it was, in fact, at the meetings of the directors that he and Morgan first became acquainted.

"But Morgan was concerned that, after his death, the bequests he intended to make to the Metropolitan might not be spent as prudently as he would have wished. It seems he had good reason for his apprehension—for there were rumors of not infrequent misappropriation of funds by officials of the Company—and so he devised an ingenious way both to safeguard his posthumous beneficence and to repay his debt to me—which, it seems, was still on his conscience. What he did was this: he added a codicil to his will bequeathing to your uncle's father the money that he had promised to pay me for the manuscript. Then, shortly before he died, he met secretly with your grandfather, told him of the intended bequest, and made one stipulation: that, within ten years of Morgan's death, your grandfather was to make every effort to arrange a production of *Salome* at the Metropolitan, with the provision that no one would ever know—even indirectly—that Morgan's money was behind it. Thus the matter would be finished: a banned opera performed, a debt paid, the Opera Company reimbursed, and no one the wiser.

"But things did not work out the way Morgan planned.

53

The Great War came, and the Metropolitan cut back on expensive new productions. Oh, there *was* talk of presenting *Salome* in the 1917–1918 season—just ten years after it had been dropped—but by November 1917 anti-German sentiments were rife, and it was announced that no German opera would be given at the Met for an indefinite period. Your grandfather, of course, knew full well that only *he* knew of Morgan's bequest and its conditions; and what he did next was—and I do not believe that I overstate the matter—base and unscrupulous. In 1921, through the British South Africa Company, he invested the money in the White Star, one of the richest copper mines in Rhodesia—it was there, you may remember, that your aunt and uncle first met a few years later." Strauss paused for a moment.

"Yes, of course." My mind was momentarily distracted from the ghost's disturbing story as my thoughts returned to tales my uncle had told me as a child about his travels in Africa. He especially enjoyed recounting how he had met my aunt, the daughter of a wealthy British mine owner; from time to time he would speak in almost mystical tones about Rhodesia, once or twice hinting that it held some private significance for his wife and her family, but he never enlightened me further on the matter.

"As it turned out," Strauss went on, "your grandfather profited very handsomely from that investment—he made close to $100,000, I've since learned—and it helped to make him a very rich man."

My shock and dismay at this revelation of my grandfather's alleged malfeasance was obvious, and I started to make some response. Strauss cut me off.

"No! I appreciate your discomfort at hearing of this sordid affair, but please let me finish. I shall soon come to the point of why I am here this evening. True, your grandfather's own money afforded him many luxuries: this grand house behind us, a magnificent collection of art and antiques, frequent trips abroad in the most opulent style. But Morgan's bequest alone—generously supplemented by the White Star investment—allowed him to buy the one sure sign of wealth and achievement he so coveted: the *Princess Melosa*. And there you have it: the *Melosa*, that splendid yacht in the harbor which we have both been admiring, and which your uncle Rhode inherited from his father, was bought with ill-gotten money, money that by all rights should have gone to a production of my opera, and some of it, eventually, to me. I do not greatly regret the financial loss; at the time, I certainly did not much need the money and was soon thereafter a very wealthy man myself. But I cannot abide the fraudulence, and the blatant dishonesty of your grandfather's act galled me. I have come to avenge that iniquity."

I knew better than to interrupt this indictment, and Strauss's voice had taken so sharp and commanding an edge that I felt it would have been unwise to say anything.

"I am not by nature an especially vindictive person and hold no brief for cruel retribution. But I do believe that punishment should fit the offense, and I intend to see that your grandfather's crime—for a crime it surely was—will at last be brought to account. Since the *Princess Melosa* was bought with tainted money—and so shamelessly (if to Latin ears mellifluously) named after the opera that financed her purchase—it is only fitting that she be sacrificed—not unlike the heroine of my opera. So take a final look at her; you will not see the *Melosa* again.''

As he spoke, my eyes had turned once again to the yacht. At first, nothing about her changed: she sat, as before, quiet and majestic on the now-still waters. Then, as I watched in horror, the *Melosa* moved: at first almost imperceptibly, then, all too clearly, her stern began to sink. After a few moments, the bow also lowered toward the water, until the gunwales were just level with the surface. Finally, and with awful speed, the *Melosa,* as though borne down by a massive weight, slipped silently beneath the surface. The once-dazzling light from her ivory-white hull still glowed from under the roiling water where she had just stood; then the light, too, was gone, and the bay lay smooth once again.

The whole dreadful scene had taken no more than a minute. Shaken and speechless, I looked beside me where Strauss had been sitting, but the ghost was gone. The gull on the nearby rock suddenly took flight, its wings moving in strong slow beats. Far off, like the attenuated wail of a clarinet, a seabird's cry rose in a plangent glissando. It was answered a few moments later by the faint mew of the gull as it glided, so low that its angled wings almost skimmed the wavelets, over the spot where the *Princess Melosa* had recently been. The birds' plaintive counterpoint, and the gentle splash of water as it lapped against the seawall, were the only sounds to be heard.

AUTHOR'S NOTE

That portion of the story concerning Strauss's *Salome* at the Metropolitan Opera, and the part Pierpont Morgan played in banning the opera's production there, is based on fact. The tale told beginning with Morgan's interest in buying Strauss's manuscript is, with few exceptions, entirely a product of the author's imagination.

The whereabouts of the autograph manuscript of Strauss's *Salome* is unknown.

The Ballad of the Belle

by her successor Nordstrom Bailey
Mark Farrell

HEN PIERPONT MORGAN heard the call
To quit this mortal scene,
He spoke his final earthly words
To Belle da Costa Greene:

"I mean to keep an eye on you
From heaven or from hell!
No man shall have what I had not!"
"That's fine with me," said Belle;

"As love has struck me from his slate,
So I my book strike clean.
No man shall foist the married state
On Belle da Costa Greene."

She dressed herself in comely weeds
    And back to work did go.
'Twas not for love, as some did say,
    But style that she did so.

She mused in sweet complacence
    As she moved from stack to stack:
"I miss the dear old rascal,
    But I do look good in black!"

A randy incunabulist
    Whose parentage was mean
Decided he would try his luck
    With Belle da Costa Greene.

He stepped into her office,
    And he closed the door behind.
She said, "I beg your pardon, sir,
    What can you have in mind?"

"It's all right. I'm a Princeton man,
    If you know what I mean."
"Indeed I do," the Belle replied.
    "How utterly duveen!

"The imbecilities I have
    To tolerate!" she said.
"You male librarians rush in
    Where Morgan feared to tread!

59

"As far as I'm concerned,
　　This tête-à-tête is at an end.
If you'll excuse me, sir,
　　I have an opera to attend."

She took her hat and coat,
　　And in the time it takes to say,
She marched out to the street
　　And caught a cab and drove away.

The saucy fellow hailed a cab
　　And followed close behind.
She spied him through her opera glass
　　And quickly closed her blind.

He sniggered in his whiskers
　　(Which he never ceased to preen):
"You haven't closed the book on me,
　　Miss Belle da Costa Greene!"

She occupied, as usual,
　　The best seat in the house.
He came and sat right down with her
　　As if she were his spouse.

"Those places are subscribed," she said.
　　He said, "That suits me fine."
"Please, sir, leave me alone," she said.
　　He said, "Your place or mine?"

60

She said, "You are no gentleman.
  You're nothing but a hoodlum.
The only way you know to deal
  With women is to doodle 'em.

"A lady should not have to use
  Her tongue, sir, as a weapon.
But you, sir, are a worm, which one
  Might use her boot to step on."

She beckoned to an usherette,
  Who showed him to his place
While Belle picked up her programme and
  Demurely fanned her face.

"So many propositions!
  I feel positively whifty!
I'll review them alphabetically
  The moment I turn fifty."

The nasty incunabulist
  Went out for a cigar
'Twas not for love: He had
  An atavistic need for tar.

And as he stood there smoking it,
  He saw—but could this be?—
Smiling to him and beckoning,
  La Belle Dame Sans Merci!

She coyly dropped her kerchief
　　As she sauntered out the door,
But all he found was laminating
　　Tissue on the floor.

He followed at a distance in
　　Another hired car
Until they reached her door, which she
　　Discreetly left ajar.

Perplexed, he went inside
　　And found her lying in her bed.
"You're just in time to join me for
　　The *Liebestod*," she said.

He told her, "I'm afraid you'll have
　　To fill me in, Miss Greene.
It's funny, but I always fell
　　Asleep before that scene."

"I'll show you, then," she said. "We'll have
　　To practice till it's right."
She drew him in beside her,
　　And she murmured in delight.

"How do you like my hair?" she said.
　　"And how do you like my skin?"
He began to understand
　　The situation he was in.

"Your hair is smooth as silk doublures.
    Your skin is soft as vellum."
"Sir, if you're fond of women,
    That is not what you should tell 'em.

"I knew a lad at Göttingen
    Who thought of girls as books.
He would have said of you,
    'He cannot read. He only looks.'

"But I will show you something which,
    Abhor it or adore it,
You can't compare with anything
    You've ever seen before it."

She peeled away her sweet pug nose
    And showed him in its place
The most hideous excrescence
    Ever formed upon a face.

"I know that nose!" he stammered
    At the thing that he had seen.
"It belongs to Pierpont Morgan,
    Not to Belle da Costa Greene!"

When Belle rolled in at two o'clock,
    She thought, "I'm getting older.
I never used to fall asleep
    At *Tristan and Isolde*."

But her face was filled with horror
 And her mind was filled with dread,
When she saw the incunabulist
 Stretched out upon her bed.

His corpse was stiff and twisted,
 But the most appalling sight
Was a scrap of silk in his left hand
 And vellum in his right!

"Untidy incunabulist
 To die upon my bed!
But—God have mercy on his soul!—
 Defenseless books to shred!"

Come, all you male librarians,
 And be advised by me:
Disport you at Delmonico's,
 But let fine maidens be.

For who can know what ill attends
 Their virginal good looks?
Better to play it safe, my friends,
 And stay in their good books.

The Clergyman's Bargain
Janet Ing Freeman

T WAS UNDERSTOOD from
the beginning that for the final editing the present
writer was to be responsible, but the responsibility
was undertaken solely in the hope and belief that it
would be shared with the friend whose loss, which
has made every day's work harder, has been especially felt in completing this last of many joint enter-
prises.

— ALFRED POLLARD, speaking of Robert Proctor in the introduction to
the *Catalogue of Manuscripts and Early Printed Books . . . Now Forming
Portion of the Library of J. Pierpont Morgan* (London, 1906–1907).

London: 28 August 1903

ROBERT PROCTOR was losing his eyesight and that, surely,
was the worst thing that could happen to a bibliographer.

He had known for years that his eyes were weakening, but had refused to think about what he would do when they finally failed. Now, as he repositioned the book he was cataloguing so that it would catch the last light coming in through the great west window of the Arch Room, he was forced to admit that no amount of twisting or turning would enable him to make out the words in the smallest of the three types.

He closed his eyes and opened them again, tried first the left on its own and then the right, but this time the old tricks didn't work. Tomorrow, he thought: tomorrow night I'll be well away from it. He touched his inside breast pocket to ensure that they were still there, the ticket from Charing Cross, the francs and the kronen. Three weeks' holiday should make the difference, he hoped: three weeks' freedom from the Museum, from the ceaseless squabbles with mother, and (most welcome of all) from the catalogue of Morgan's books. And when he returned he would stand firm. Pollard and Duff would simply have to finish the project without him, and the money be damned.

Around him the others were beginning to put away their pens, search for their hats and packages. Proctor gathered his own things up, carefully placing a flat parcel in his bag. The letter to Pollard was already written, begging his colleague to accept the completed descriptions but to excuse him from further participation in the American enterprise. He would post it on the way home, and send the catalogue entries tomorrow. There now remained only one more task before leaving for Austria: Robert Proctor had to lay a ghost.

Leaving the Museum he crossed into Bedford Square and blinked again in the late August sun. He clutched his bag more tightly and walked briskly west, zig-zagging left and right from one narrow street to another. How could he have known that a ten-minute detour between here and Paddington would cause all this trouble? Why had he ever listened to Streatfeild?

"You mean you've never visited Dibdin's church?" his friend had cried. "But you simply *must*! A quite charming Smirke, lovely yellowy colour, sure to be marvellous this time of year." The time had been April, and it had sounded like a good use of a few minutes en route to the Oxford train, really not out of the way at all. Proctor had little sympathy for the Reverend T. F. Dibdin, apostle of bibliomaniacs nearly a century before (imagine going to *that* chatterbox for spiritual advice, he had thought with a hrmph), but a good piece of ecclesiastical architecture was always worth the extra steps.

And St. Mary's hadn't disappointed. As Streatfeild had warned, the interior was a bit dim, but the simple columned portico and round tower had delighted Proctor. Very well sited, he thought, looking south into Bryanston Square and then north at the church. Very nice indeed. Satisfied, he turned again toward Crawford Street and Paddington Station, but before he could take half a dozen steps a voice stopped him.

"How do you like my church, sir?" it asked. Proctor looked around. Yes, there he was—a plump old man sitting on a bench to one side of the forecourt. The rector, he thought, and then revised his estimate as he looked more closely at the man: a former rector, surely, and one who had carefully saved his grandfather's clothes for his own last years. That kind of hat hasn't been made for fifty years or more, and the cravat.... Proctor shook these thoughts away and acknowledged the man, hurriedly tossing off a remark about the architecture and the play of blue sky and clouds behind the cupola.

"Always draughty during the service, though," the old man said with a touch of petulance. "And so little light I could hardly read my sermons. Oh my eyes, my eyes—I did think they would go before I convinced the Churchwardens (dear and good friends that they were) that more candles were needed."

"I sympathize with you, sir," Proctor said automatically, thinking more of his train than the conversation. "My own eyes have been weak since I was at school, and recently I fear added work has strained them even more."

"What is your work, sir, if I may ask? You do not have the bearing of a solicitor (a profession I myself abandoned when young, I might add). Your parcel suggests some small folios —are you perhaps a bookseller, or a literary man yourself?"

"Assistant Keeper at the British Museum, sir, taking

these volumes to Oxford to compare with some in the Bodleian Library. And—if you will excuse me—I must hurry to catch my train."

But the old clergyman was persistent, and Proctor, though sighing with impatience, was nonetheless too polite to refuse him a glimpse of the books. As he unwrapped them a single sheet fluttered to the bench, the sight of it sending his companion into a near swoon: "This must certainly be the work of William Caxton: O venerable and virtuous typographer, may his name be held in reverence! And—yes, here is her name—it can only be a leaf from the most excessively rare *Lyf of Saynt Wenefryde*, the history of that Welsh maiden of fair countenance from whose spring flow forth the curative waters!"

Really, thought Proctor as the man began to intone the text, what nonsense (venerable and virtuous typographer, indeed!). He's obviously been reading too much Dibdin in his retirement—I should imagine there'll be a whole set of his works on the rectory shelves. Still, Proctor had to admit that the old boy knew something about books, and despite his complaints his eyes were well up to the quirks of Caxton's Number Four type.

"...gyvyng laude to almyghty god in his grete and merveylous werkes," the rector finished up triumphantly. "Most magnificent, my dear sir, truly splendid! I see this wrapper is marked 'Morgan'—would that be the bookseller (not one known to me) from whom you obtained this jewel?"

Restraining himself with difficulty from snatching the

leaf away and returning it to his parcel, Proctor corrected him, describing the rich American who had purchased hundreds of fifteenth-century books and commissioned a grand catalogue of the collection. "My friend Pollard at the Museum is in charge of the project, and I've agreed to do some of the entries. But, as I mentioned"— and here Proctor wondered how he had got into such a personal discussion with a stranger, clergyman or not—"my eyes are growing steadily worse, and I doubt that I shall be able to complete my share of the work."

"Perhaps, sir, I could then be of some small assistance. It has been some years now since I have taken up my pen in bibliophilic pursuits, but I may say without undue pretence that in my day there was no one more willing to undertake that happy toil. I should be glad indeed once again to handle such curiosities and pleased to help so sympathetic a young man as yourself."

So the arrangement had been made. Pollard had already agreed that Proctor could do most of the cataloguing at home, carrying the smaller books to Oxshott and working at them evenings and weekends. Now Proctor saw that this plan could easily accommodate a stop in Marylebone, where he could avail himself of the old rector's seeming expertise in transcription. "They allow me the occasional use of a room in the rectory," his new friend had said, "though as I do not wish to discommode the present incumbent I prefer only to occupy it whilst the family are engaged at their evening meal and amusements."

The room had proved to be a cramped study at the back of the house, intended perhaps as a curate's refuge, and conveniently provided with a door into the mews behind the rectory. Over the next weeks a routine had developed: Proctor would arrive with his carpet-bag full of books at seven, and before he could raise his hand to knock, the door would open. Book by book the two men would work through the stack, the old clergyman reading out the text to Proctor and, to the latter's occasional distress, discoursing on the typography or decoration in a manner worthy indeed of the inimitable Dibdin. Yes, I was right, thought Proctor, spotting the row of that author's books in a place of honour: he's memorized every word ever written by his hero.

Promptly at ten the old man would stop, clearly eager to vacate the study before someone might come in. I wonder where he lives himself, Proctor thought once or twice, but as the clergyman seemed well-fed enough he saw no real cause for concern. Absorbed in his own work, he did not even find it odd that the old man had refused to give his name. "Doctor will do, sir," he had said the first night, "just Doctor." And with a laugh he had moved off across the dark forecourt, disappearing into the shadows around the church as Proctor peered after him.

Lost in thoughts of the past few months, Robert Proctor stepped off the kerb without looking and was forced to jump back as a horse-drawn omnibus thundered past. Baker Street, he realized: nearly at St. Mary's. Brought back to the present, he was reminded as he waited to cross of a bit of literary gossip he had heard that day at the Museum. One of the other Assistants had had it from a cousin who wrote for the *Strand*, who had claimed that Conan Doyle had finally consented to bring Holmes back to life in the October number. Mother will like *that*, thought Proctor, recalling the debates he had had with her after "The Final Problem" had appeared in 1893. As one among many readers who regarded Holmes and Watson as real people, Mrs. Proctor had been greatly distressed by the detective's plunge into the Reichenbach Falls, but Proctor himself (who preferred Henry James but dutifully read Conan Doyle aloud when requested) judged it a clever way to finish off a tiresome character. I really must go there myself, he thought: perhaps on next year's jaunt.

Proctor hurried up Crawford Street and turned into the mews, anxious for his task to be behind him. He shuddered as he remembered the evening just a week before, when he and the old rector had finished up the last of the French books. "I don't know how to thank you," he had said. "If it does not offend, perhaps you will accept some portion of the fee Morgan is paying for my work."

"Do not dare to think of it, my dear man," had been the reply as the rector turned his attention to Proctor's stack of descriptions, fussing over them while the other man repacked the books. "Money is nothing to me now."

Taking him at his word, Proctor had not insisted, but had waited impatiently for the old man to return the bulky sheaf of descriptions. I suppose I should have handed some of them over already, he had thought, but Pollard is always so busy, and now he's off on holiday. As he glanced down at the papers a final time, Proctor suddenly froze. The top sheet, which should have been covered with a detailed account of the 1471 Sallust, was blank. He looked quickly at the second sheet, then the third, and in panic began to tear through the pile, searching for any writing whatsoever.

"They're all blank!" he had cried. "My god, has it happened? Have my eyes finally gone?" But he had immediately realized that that was not the problem, for he could see the smiling old clergyman as clearly as he ever had. "Tell me, sir," he had begged, "am I going mad?"

While Proctor watched, the other man's smile slowly turned to a self-satisfied laugh. "Remarkable, isn't it?" he had said. "A most amazing thing I learned from a Chinese magician who once came to entertain His Lordship. A simple powder (simple, though the ingredients are not easily found outside Cathay), a casual dusting, and anything written in the ink from the pot on that desk disappears at once! But look, sir," he had demanded, pulling a small phial from his coat pocket, "when I apply this second powder the writing reappears as if never dispersed!" It was true: with a light application of the fine grains the description of the Sallust had returned to the sheet.

"It is witchcraft," exclaimed Proctor, "and you, sir, are no clergyman but the very devil!" There must be some way out of this nightmare, he had thought in panic: perhaps I didn't offer him enough. "I've been promised seventy-five pounds for my work thus far—it's all yours, all of it."

"Money can buy me nothing now," the old man had repeated, "for I am far beyond the need of earthly comforts. Tell me, young man, have you truly no idea who has been doing your work for you these past months?" He drew himself up and struck a pose. "It is I—Thomas Frognall Dibdin!"

Dibdin himself. A distant part of Proctor's brain told him it couldn't be, but the bibliographer was beyond rational thought. In a frenzy he turned to the other, promising anything in return for the restored descriptions. I can't do them over, he thought: Quaritch have already packed the books for shipment to America. "Anything," he said again, "anything."

"Ah, well, there is one trifle, such a small thing. The millionaire Morgan will never miss it (if he looks at his treasures at all!), but it would bring me great pleasure in this cold existence. I refer, of course, to the leaf of Caxton's *Saynt Wenefryde*."

"But it's impossible! The leaf is irreplaceable, and anyway Duff has taken it off to Manchester for the summer with the other English books."

"You will find a way, I do not doubt; and as you will not wish to delay your departure for the Tyrol, I suggest we meet here once more a week from today. Meanwhile I shall keep the papers—and my little phials—safe from harm." Then, holding tight to the descriptions, he had vanished, leaving behind nothing but the memory of a smile.

The old clergyman was smiling again now as Proctor put the Caxton leaf into his eager hands. "Such a treasure," he said in his boring way, "and one far too magnificent for a philistine American! *I* shall know how to savour it fully, and it shall not ever leave my side! But now—your papers." He reached behind him and took out the stack of descriptions. Proctor thumbed through them in haste—yes, all there, a bit faded perhaps, but quite legible. "I thank you, sir," he said tersely, putting them into his bag and going to the door. "I shall be off now, for I still have much to do before my journey."

What a relief! he thought on the way back to the Baker Street bus. I've got away with it, and as long as Jacobi says nothing, Duff won't even need to know the leaf ever left my hands last week: by now the original will be safely back in Manchester, and the type for the facsimile broken down. In his elation Proctor was already beginning to forget the ghostly rector and the horrors of the hours that had followed their meeting the previous Friday, when he had returned to Oxshott in a daze and gone straight to his study, locking himself in against his mother's offers of cocoa. There he had remained until dawn, struggling both with the evidence that he had seen a ghost and with the temptation to do as Dibdin had asked.

Finally, pacing between one bookshelf and another, he had accepted the apparition for what it had been. But I cannot do it, he thought: I shall have to tell Pollard I have lost the descriptions, and if it means the end of our friendship,

I will deserve it. With a sigh he had turned to the nearest shelf, seeking consolation among the neat rows of books. One of Morris's sagas would be soothing—something printed in a good black type on fine paper. Proctor reached for the first in the series of plain vellum spines that marked his late friend's productions, and in the instant he put out his hand the plan was complete in his mind. It just may work, he had thought, opening the book and looking down not at one of Morris's own types, but at a near perfect re-creation of Caxton's Number Four. *"Gunnlaug the Worm-Tongue and Raven the Skald,"* he read, "printed at the Chiswick Press for William Morris, 1891."

Yes, Jacobi had made a remarkable job of it, Proctor thought now as he squeezed into a seat on the crowded bus. The most painstaking composition directly from the original, hastily recalled from a somewhat puzzled Duff; the finest black ink; the discreet touches of pen; and (Jacobi's triumph) a dingy sheet of seventeenth-century paper. "Old Whittingham himself could not have done better," the Press director had boasted, talking of the time a half century before when that printer had commissioned the facsimile fount and used it to print leaves to "complete" Caxtons in the stocks of Pickering and Stevens. "Now, a bit of judicious crumpling and soiling, and I am sure you will win your bet with your friend: he will not be able to tell the original from the copy, I swear it!" Beaming with satisfaction and the prospect of ten guineas, Jacobi had affectionately patted the case of type.

"Back to the basement with this, I'm afraid. And now, as you're here, let me have your opinion on this new specimen of Greek from Chiswell Street...."

All behind me now, thought Proctor, standing up ready to leap off at his stop: and three weeks of solitude ahead.

Near the Tashnach Glacier: 6 September 1903
For the first time since morning Robert Proctor had stopped for a sandwich and a sip of brandy. He looked around, once again glad he had come alone. He knew he was a good enough Alpinist to cross to the next hut on his own, and because of his eyes he was taking more care than usual. *Not* to the right, he thought now, poking at the ice with his stick and noting the beginnings of a crevasse. Straight on for a bit, he decided, and a few more hours will find me in front of a warm fire. He put away his flask and stretched, eager to be off again, but suddenly he was no longer alone on the glacier.

"Ha! Proctor! Stop!" He knew the voice, knew before he turned that it could be no one else. And then the old clergyman was beside him, waving his stick in one hand and the Caxton leaf in the other. "You tried to trick me," he cried, "but it *won't work!* You thought you were so clever, young fellow, but however you did it, you overlooked one thing. Just look at this watermark: tell me, when did you last see *that* on fifteenth-century paper?"

Damning Jacobi in his mind, Proctor peered at the sheet, desperately seeking the mark. At long last the sun picked out the faint contours of a Strasbourg lily and Proctor sighed. Yes, he thought: like Holmes I seem to have underestimated my adversary.

"You are correct, sir," he said quietly, "but I am afraid there is nothing to be done now." And still holding the leaf he turned right, tears in his nearly blind eyes, towards a ledge unindicated on Alpine charts.

Oxshott: 5 October 1903

Alfred Pollard hesitated on the steps as the door of "Midgarth" closed behind him. It had clearly been his duty to take the news to Proctor's mother, but he was far more shaken than he had anticipated. Early that morning Streatfeild had returned from his hurried journey to the Tyrol; exhausted, he had given his report to a silent audience. "No sign of him at all," he had said. "I have checked everywhere, but no one saw him after he left the hut where he spent the night of the fifth. I am very much afraid there is small hope of his being still alive."

Pollard had gone straight to Oxshott, prepared to comfort his friend's mother as he took from her what he imagined would be the last crumbs of hope. Finding her by the sitting room fire, he advanced with outstretched hands, murmuring the conventional words. "Mrs. Proctor," he began, "I am so sorry—" But here Pollard had stopped in confusion, for on the old woman's face was a radiant smile. Has she somehow had good news, he thought with a rush of joy. If only it could be so!

"Mr. Pollard, how nice of you to visit," she said, putting down the latest *Strand* and crossing the room to him, "though I regret it may be some time before Robert returns. Surely the Museum will not want him to cut short his travels in Tibet with Sherlock Holmes!" Pollard stared at her in amazement as her words sank in: she's completely gone, he thought, it's turned her mind and there is nothing I can do. "Mrs. Proctor," he had begun again, "perhaps we could sit down...."

Now, an hour later, it was over—the old woman taken to bed by her maid, and Pollard able at last to return to the Museum. In his mind was only one consolation. At least she will never have to know that Proctor did not finish his last job, he thought, for I shall credit him with it nonetheless, as a memorial to our friendship these many years. But really, he wondered for the hundredth time, whatever could have possessed my unfortunate colleague to send me a packet full of blank paper in the place of those descriptions?

Non Furtum Facies
Richard Priest

ILLIAM BÜCHER was proud of his collection of Aldines. It was almost complete up to 1529, the year in which Andreas Torresanus, Aldus's father-in-law and the second operator of the press, died. Only two incunables were missing: the Greek *Horae* and the Reuchlin. The latter was so rare that Bücher didn't know the location of a single copy. It was not listed in the catalogues of the British Museum, the Bibliothèque Nationale, or the John Rylands Library, nor in Proctor's Index, and no copy was recorded in either the American or Italian census of incunabula. A footnote in Renouard's bibliography of Aldines indicated that there might be a copy in Munich.

The Morgan Library had four copies of the *Horae,* which Bücher thought rather unfair, since he had not been able to acquire even one. Hence, he decided to steal one of the

Morgan copies. Bücher was an essentially honest man. In the course of amassing a large fortune, he had ruined only six persons, not one of them as a result of malice, pettiness, or caprice, and he had employed no actually illegal methods. Stealing a book would be a break with the past, but he felt that the Morgan could well afford to give up one of its copies to him. The variants in the Morgan copies had been carefully described in the literature, so there would be no real loss to the world of scholarship.

He planned the theft with great care. The book was small enough to fit into the side pocket of his jacket, and he would not be subject to a body search upon leaving the Reading Room. All he had to do was to turn in an acceptable substitute for the volume he was stealing. He studied papermaking, procured linen rags, and manufactured paper which was very close to that used by Aldus. A microfilm of the text was obtained, but from another library in order to reduce the probability that he would be suspected, if the theft were discovered. Working from full-size prints made from the microfilm, Bücher created a facsimile using methods of his own devising. A microfilm of another book with the same Morgan Library bookplate was procured to facilitate duplication of that item. Reproducing the binding was the most difficult feat of all, since he thought it better not to ask for photographs of the covers and spine. The final result of all this effort was superb. Detection of the forgery could come from only a very close examination.

Before leaving home on the day of the projected theft,

The Reading Room

Bücher received a package from a bookseller. Since he had not ordered anything from that dealer recently, his curiosity could hardly be contained. It had to be something so desirable that the dealer had sent it to him without asking if it might be sent on approval. To open or not to open, that was the question. If the contents were very exciting, it might affect the steadiness of hand which he would require in effecting the substitution. He decided to wait until later to open the package.

Bücher arrived at the library just after the Reading Room opened. He knew from experience that he would probably be the only reader at that hour and that only one member of the staff was likely to be present. Since he had filed the call slip the day before, the book was produced promptly. When the librarian's back was turned, Bücher reached for the original with his right hand while moving his other hand toward the left pocket of his jacket to remove the facsimile. Suddenly, an agonizing pain shot through his right arm, which then became completely paralyzed. His cry of pain caused the librarian to turn around and look at him inquiringly. Bücher realized that circumstances now rendered further attempts at substitution impractical. After telling the librarian he wasn't feeling well, he left.

On his way from the Reading Room to the outer door of the library, Bücher decided to abandon the whole idea of a theft. It seemed a prudent decision. As he began to descend the short flight of steps leading to the sidewalk, he was passed by a lady also going down the steps. Turning around, she looked directly at him, and although her lips did not move and he heard no sound, he *knew* that she said to him, "It was indeed a prudent decision, Mr. Bücher." The lady's face was familiar. He had seen it recently in a painting or photograph. His heart skipped a beat as he remembered the identity of the person depicted therein. But that was impossible, wasn't it? Miss Greene, the first director of the Morgan Library, had been dead some twenty years. He returned to the door and asked the guard, whom he knew to be both knowledgeable and observant, about the identity of the lady who had just left the library. The guard looked surprised and said, "Mr. Bücher, no one has gone through this door since you did."

When he got home, Bücher was feeling somewhat better. He was slowly beginning to regain the use of his right arm. Although he usually drank only wine, he decided to have an extra-dry double martini to steady his nerves. Turning his attention to the package which had arrived earlier that day, he removed a letter that was attached to the outside and read it.

Dear Mr. Bücher,
Some time ago, you asked me to look out for a leaf of the Gutenberg Bible which is more interesting from the textual point of view than the leaf you already possess. I am therefore taking the liberty of sending you on approval leaf 38 from volume I. The text runs from Exodus 18:25 to 21:10. The price may seem high, but

I am sure you realize that this leaf is one of the most desirable since it contains Exodus 20. Furthermore, as indicated on the invoice, I am willing to make a generous allowance against the price if you wish to trade in your present leaf which I understand is from the book of Zacharias....

Bücher had always hoped to acquire the leaf containing I Timothy 5:23. Also high on his list were Genesis 1, Psalm 22, and Matthew 5. Suddenly, he broke out into a cold sweat when he remembered the content of Exodus 20. No, Exodus 20 simply would not do. He immediately re-addressed the package, took it to the post office, and mailed it back to the dealer.

After lunch, during which he steadied his nerves still further with a bottle of Mouton Rothschild 1929, he decided to read his Gutenberg Bible leaf. He had always assumed it to be rather uninteresting, but maybe it was better than he thought. The text, which began with Zacharias 1:12, generally confirmed his assumption until he reached the second column on the verso, where he read in Chapter 5: *Haec est maledictio quae egreditur super faciem omnis terrae; quia omnis fur sicut ibi scriptum est judicabitur.*

As a result of these nerve-shattering events, Bücher soon lost interest in rare books, and he sold his entire collection. Since he gave up reading catalogues, he was unaware that the Morgan Library sold one of its four copies of the Greek *Horae* at public auction one year later.

The Aldine edition of Reuchlin's *Oratio pro Philippo Bavariae* is very rare indeed, but there are copies in Munich, Stuttgart, and Zurich. Giorgio Uzielli's copy is listed in the supplement to the American census of incunabula which had not yet appeared at the time the events in this story took place. This copy is now at the University of Texas. The rarity of the Greek *Horae* is noted by Dibdin: "It is perhaps not too much to affirm, that the present is the *Rarest Aldine volume* which exists," and by a Sotheby cataloguer: "*The rarest of all the early Aldines.*" However, the *Horae* is not so rare as the Reuchlin; there are ten copies in the American census, five in the Italian census, and there are copies in the British, Bodleian, and Rylands Libraries.

It is appropriate to note here that one supposed fifteenth-century Aldine, Politian's *La giostra di Giuliano de' Medici* (Copinger 4808), as listed by Burger, is a bibliographical ghost.

Slide Lecture
Liran Ludeley

OU AREN'T LATE. Not a bit.
I went up to the library to browse around and lost track of
time myself. Lovely to see you. Now, what will you have?
I'll have a Club Special, please. You have that too. Two
kinds of rum, and some fruit juice, and sugar, and so on.
It's tasty. I think you'll find it tasty.

I was looking over the new books by members, and I
found this. Here it is, all properly checked out and so forth:
I wouldn't neglect that. Now I was interested to see a biography of her. Member of the Club, you know. She was a
fascinating woman. An ideal subject for biography, really.
I mean: early life, divorce, continued education, writings,
and then she married what's his name, the Nobel Laureate,
and then won two herself. And so picturesque, too. Here's
a photo of her, in a dress she made herself, I think. You can

always tell, can't you? And here he is with her. Doesn't look like much, does he? Literature was her subject, not men. It's a lot, isn't it. She was a member of this Club, too—did I tell you that? My husband's Aunt Mary knew her slightly, years and years ago. Here we are. Well, cheers. That's tasty, isn't it? She was interested because of the Morgan Library connection, too. Not only was she the most ardent blue-stocking—Aunt Mary, I mean—but she had worked there briefly. Just a couple of years, in Prints and Drawings.

That's right. Worked under the great Felice. Yes, indeed. In fact, it was partly because of her that she became a member of the Club—Aunt Mary, I'm talking about now—and through her that I did, so my membership goes right back three respectable generations, you might say. No, I don't know who sponsored Elizabeth Wharton. Might be interesting to find out. Or maybe it's in the book. A thing like that would be important. Probably she was elected without much opposition. I mean, *two* Nobel Prizes, and all those happy children, and having saved him from suicide all those times. What? Oh, you're probably right. Not in the membership proposal.

And I can tell you what won't be in the biography: the most crucial thing in her adult life. The ghosts.

Of course, I'm sure that's not in the book. After all, this is the twenty-first century. We don't believe in ghosts, do we? I mean, St. Matthew didn't write at the dictation of an *angel*, did he? It was the apostle at the next desk throwing his voice.

I take it seriously, though. Furthermore, Aunt Mary took it seriously, too, which is remarkable. She was a complete rationalist. Complete. Had her clothes arranged by color in the closets. Understood magnetism, and so forth. But I heard her tell the story many times, and I can tell you she took it seriously. Maybe knowing the Library so well had something to do with it. I don't know. Are you ready for another of those? No? Well, just one this time, thank you.

It happened to Elizabeth Wharton, as she later styled herself, and her first husband. He's in the book, of course. Tony Lloyd. A nobody, really. Oh, I've no doubt the writer heard all about it, doing her researches, and she threw it right out. That isn't the way history is written these days, is it? That isn't the way it's deconstructed. I lay it in the lap of those Frenchmen fifty years ago, and they weren't interested in ghosts, were they? Just in morgue lists and wool trade records and so forth. Here we are. Thank you. Sure you're not ready yet? Tasty.

Well, then, let me see. She was married to the first husband, and he was then writing a book, and he was due to give the Ryskamp Lecture at the Morgan Library. Oh, yes: he had a future then. He was the dominant partner in the marriage, no doubt about it. She had dropped out of school to marry, I think—I'll have to look it up—and was helping him with his research, and he'd been at it a year or more, and had the book ready to go, and the important thing was that he had proof, or so he said, or so, at any rate, the Library believed—proof of the Big Rumor. You know. The rumor about the founder and the first director.

No, Ryskamp was later. He was number three or four. Before he went on to the Frick and so forth. Aunt Mary knew him, as a matter of fact, but she didn't know the first director. Missed her by a few years. Anyway, he had been working—Tony Lloyd had—on the origins of the collections and the lives of the founder and the directors and so forth, and it was winter, and he was to give this lecture to a roomful of Fellows and Trustees and all the people who would come to a lecture like that, but in spite of the Library's reputation there was considerable excitement about *this* lecture, because of its salacious possibilities. The press was coming and so forth. People then cared a lot about the press. It was before the great libel trials of the 'Nineties.

Sweet scandal. That's what it was to be. Sensation. Nothing like it at the Morgan Library since the Spanish Forger case. Now *that* was a scandal, by the way. Anyway, here was something to blow the lid off the most sacred of relationships, that between a bibliophile and his librarian. Decorously, of course. A decorous flash of undergarments for the delight of connoisseurs. To prove—what? That no bastion is safe, I guess.

Aunt Mary wasn't there. She said later that she intended to go, its being the sensation of the year and so forth, but that she went shopping for her nephews' Christmas and forgot about it, but I think that was her way of working the family into the story. I'm not even sure she was in New York at the time. Anyway, she retained a keen interest in

The Entrance

Library activities, that was true, and certainly in Library gossip, and she kept her glass to the wall, so to speak. However she learned it, she knew a lot about it. A lot.

It was winter, one of those cold, sloppy days when the city streets were full of roaring, heaving traffic, pneumatic doors sighing open and closed on busses, squealing brakes, hissing and crunching, and steam rising out of the pavement, and people stepping off the curbs into icy puddles, cursing under their breaths. You get the picture. One of the Library guards was outside, with his arms crossed, hands in his armpits, getting a breath of air, jiggling from foot to foot, and he saw the Lloyds, as they then were, coming along, wrapped, no doubt, in those inflatable coats people wore then, carrying the sort of things people carried: tote bags, shoulder bags (I have one of Aunt Mary's, believe it or not, in lovely condition, museum quality, really, with "Thirteen" written all over it), folders of notes, boxes of those old celluloid slides they had. Probably even some clean shoes in a bag.

And Elizabeth was haranguing him about something, begging him to do something, or, one may suppose, not to do it.

Coming along toward the Library, then, uneventfully, until the man, Tony, was almost run down by a taxi screaming along up Madison Avenue. Or down, whichever it was in those days. Up. I'm sure you're right. And if you can remember which way the traffic ran on Madison Avenue fifty years ago, you must need another drink. Yes? Well, I'll keep you company. Two more of the same. Thank you.

Notebooks flew everywhere, and the two of them were clutching loose pages, and she was wiping off the back of his trousers when they reached the Library.

"That was a bat out of hell!" Tony Lloyd said.

And Elizabeth said, "Somebody ought to report him."

And Tony said again, "A bat out of hell!"

The guard heard him.

Cheers. So they went crunching up the steps in those rubber shoes, and the guard followed them. He heard Elizabeth Lloyd, as I'll call her for clarity, say something about "Pierpont Peyton Place," as she pushed through the turnstile, and when her husband tried to follow, the thing stuck. There he was, with his fists full of tote bags and papers, keeping the wet ones away from the dry ones, knocking backwards and forwards with his thighs uselessly until Elizabeth said, "Tony, for heaven's sake!" and gave the thing a bang with the heel of her hand, whereupon it turned with a vengeance, throwing Tony into the foyer of the Library and his notes all over the floor. With a vengeance. Literally. There were two or three guards around and a civilian volunteer taking up tolls, and they all watched while Elizabeth checked her husband for bruises and helped him pick up the pages.

"You're sure you're all right?" Elizabeth asked as they crossed the foyer.

"Fine, fine," Tony said vaguely. "Lucky the pages are numbered. That's all." He was shuffling papers as he walked, turning them this way and that.

"Well, if you ..." she began, when Tony exploded.

"They're not! Holy smoke, look at that! They're not numbered! Oh, Honey...three copies! Sixty pages!"

They had both stopped walking.

"Calm down," Elizabeth said. "They are numbered! I did it myself. You just checked it on the bus, remember? Calm down, Tony."

"Well, there's sure as hell no number *there*, is there? Or there?" He poked the corners of the pages under her nose, then pulled them away. "Egyptian antiquities. That's way along. Princes Gate. Where are we now? Wait a minute, here's Pierpont's death." He spoke to himself.

"Well, the Xerox must have cut off one or two corners," she said hastily, but then added, "No, that's not right. I numbered them by hand. Tony, maybe I missed some." She leaned over to look at the pages with him. "Look, we'll get it all straightened out in the Meeting Room. You know these by heart anyway. It won't matter." Her tone was less than confident.

The door of the staff elevator was open, inviting, as they approached, but Tony took Elizabeth's elbow and stopped, with a look on his face that said something wasn't right, and he pulled her toward the stairs.

"This'll be faster," he said, in response to her puzzled look. He tucked the folders under an arm, and reached to unhook the heavy velvet cordon blocking the stairs. A blue bolt of light flashed between the hook and its ring, there was a sound like a firecracker, and Tony dropped the cordon and shook his hand.

"Good Lord!" Elizabeth exclaimed. "Are you all right?" And when he didn't reply, sucking his middle fingers, she said, "Do you smell sulfur?"

He looked past her, up the stairs, with a grim face. "No," he said, and pushed forward, both of them skirting the cordon, which lay on the bottom step, poised to strike.

"Is brass a conductor?" Elizabeth asked as they mounted the stairs.

"What?" Tony asked.

"I don't think brass is a conductor," she said.

"What? Sure it is. They make light bulb filaments out of it," he said hastily.

"No, they don't!" she said, frowning at him.

"Velvet is the conductor," he said, and they walked through the short corridor, its vitrines filled with evocative photographs in preparation for his lecture, into the empty Meeting Room.

By the way, Tony Lloyd was wearing rubber overshoes. I can see you're ready for another, and I'll keep you company. And by the way, later that day the staff elevator did drop six inches of its own accord. The door was open. No one aboard, of course. They said that something got into the cables. Static electricity or something. That's what they said.

Well, now, in the Meeting Room that fateful day the screen was lowered at the front of the room, and Tony strode toward it, through seats for more than two hundred people. He barely paused at the front of the room but leaped onto the stage, his notes clutched against his side, to stand at the podium. Elizabeth followed, and stood at the front of the audience, looking up. There was the podium, the microphone, a water glass, a tensor light, and a button for signalling a change of slides, all arranged like instruments of the Passion. High in the back wall of the room, Tony could see the black snout of the projector inside the booth, lighted, silent, and waiting.

"I'm putting these in order," Tony said grimly, making it sound like a threat. He began slipping papers in and out of piles, silently. Elizabeth heaved the tote bag onto the apron of the stage, opened it, and removed two cases of slides.

"I'll take these back to her," she said.

"Who?" Tony demanded, looking up.

Elizabeth met his eyes innocently. "Who what?" she asked.

"You said you'd give them to *her*. To whom?"

"I said I'll take the slides back there. I'll give them to whoever's going to show them."

"That wasn't what you said."

"Of course it was!"

"Sure. Right," he said resentfully, and went back to sorting papers. While she carried the slides away from him, he made three neat stacks of pages, tapping the edges, and put two of them together on top of his empty folder, tapping them all again. He set the third stack neatly in the middle of the lectern and stepped back to admire it. Easing back two more careful paces, he tapped the air gently with the folder and his duplicates, held in both hands, and said inaudibly, "There. There. Stay there."

Sidling away from the podium, staring superstitiously at his notes as though to fix them there, he said to Elizabeth when she returned, "Did you do it?"

"Do what?" she said in exasperation.

"Did you hand them in?"

"Of course," she said.

"Did somebody take them?" he asked.

"No, they refused them!" she exclaimed. "Of course they took them. The door opened a crack, and the slides were whisked efficiently inside. Greedily, as a matter of fact."

Tony looked back at the rectangle which marked the projection booth, and said, "As if by magic."

"To coin a phrase," said Elizabeth. "Tony, you have got the worst case of stage fright I have ever seen. I don't suppose they've got an ounce of scotch in this place."

"I don't need any scotch," he said, as he started to leap off the stage and then, thinking better of it, walked down the steps. "I need to see my slides through once, and then I need to go through the lecture." He settled himself in the middle of the first row, with his folder and papers on the seat next to him. When Elizabeth started to sit down, he said, "No, Honey, please, you sit about halfway back. See how they look. That's right. Anywhere there is O.K."

So the audience of two turned their backs on that unseen

projectionist, and settled down.

"First slide!" Tony called.

Nothing happened.

He leaned forward in his seat, and called out again, facing the stage, "First slide, please!"

Still nothing.

He turned toward the back of the room, and directing his gaze and his voice upward blindly he called out, "Excuse me, could we have the room lights down, and the first slide on the screen, please?"

There was a pause, and the room went completely dark, except for the light in the projection booth. Through the entrance door, Tony could see the corridor and the vitrines in light, and then that door swung to with a considerable whoosh.

Later, the guard who worked the public elevator said he found the door jammed shut and heard some funny noises in the Meeting Room, as though the mike were on the fritz, and someone shouting, as if the lecturer were mad at the microphone, very naturally. The guard went to find a maintenance man to help, and by the time they got back things were pretty much over. So the next part of the story you may take or leave. Two more Specials here, please.

"Well, that's better, I guess," said Elizabeth into the darkness.

Tony settled back into his seat, with darkness pressing in around him, and no one could have seen him jerk when a beam of projector light cut through the air like a laser sword, and the screen was blinding white.

"All *right*," said Elizabeth behind him.

Tony said again, "First slide, please."

A bass-baritone said, "No!"

After a second or so, Tony said softly, "Elizabeth?"

When it came again, the voice filled the room. "No! No! No!" accompanied by loud thumpings.

Tony found himself shaking his head from side to side as though to clear away the darkness.

"Lies! Lies! Lies!" roared the voice. "Rubbish! Confounded rubbish!"

"Who *is* that?" Tony asked hopelessly, and the room became darker still, for the white glare on the screen was replaced with black and white, a photographic portrait projected twice life size. There was a glint from the watch chain and a glint from one of the pitiless eyes, and beefy hands grasping as though someone had threatened to repossess the armchair. The mouth was mostly hidden by the famous moustache.

"No," Tony said bravely, almost conversationally. "That's wrong. That's not the first one...."

But the giant stayed on the screen, and as the two people stared, the light must have flickered, because it seemed that the watch chain sparkled and the eye wetly gleamed, and a draught must have disturbed the screen, because it seemed that breath moved the buttons of the waistcoat. They stared, and the giant stared back implacably, and as they watched the right hand rose and fell upon the arm of the chair, a gesture of controlled fury. There was a sound like a pound of sirloin dropped upon a hardwood floor, and at this signal an isosceles flame seized the bottom of the slide, licked upward, grew, splitting the image in two, and the slide was consumed before their eyes.

The screen was blazing white again, and Tony sat forward and exclaimed, "Now wait a minute! The fool has destroyed my Steichen slide! Elizabeth, who the hell is..."

The next slide was the yacht *Corsair*, and Tony had time to say, "Now that's more like..." before it too took fire and melted.

"Hold it!" he cried out in protest, but upon the screen came Princes Gate, the house, and burned; and then an interior of Princes Gate, which burned; and then another portrait. This one was a poetic study of the lady, dressed by Fortuny in the infinite glossy pleats of the neo-Hellenes, captured by De Meyer, and the grayer tongue licked up across the gray figure, and it was gone. A head study of the lady, dusky, exotic, near full face, the jaw expertly shadowed, was gone in milliseconds.

The beam on the screen seemed animated then by humid writhings which, like microscopic protozoa, slid and jittered, and a cloud-like smoke blown into the projector's beam passed through it, or in front of it, and began to collect. It seemed to want to solidify, like a film of the universal Big Bang run backwards, at increasing speed.

A figure formed, the body round and long, the head a mass of coarse and lambent hair, with light behind it like a halo. Tony put his hot hands, which he could not see, over his face, and took them away again. The figure was covered in spongy, smoky pleats like the underside of a mushroom, the hair massed and piled upon the head, and dark, but not darker than the holes where eyes should have been. Light glowed everywhere, passing through the figure, but those two umbrous smudges were opaque and black as Plato's cave.

A sound commenced, as though the microphone had been turned on, a screeching whistle known to any lecturer, increasing in volume, slowly, slowly, until Tony covered his ears and he, like Elizabeth, unseen behind him, involuntarily began to crouch down in his seat, his face a mask of agony.

"Stop it!" he cried uselessly into the din, throwing his voice against the shriek.

Then the figure on the screen began to raise one vaporous arm, and from her terrible mouth came terrible words, "Eat them! You will eat your words!" The voice was the moan of a soul disturbed in death, the voice of one who spins within her grave, disturbs her wrappings, and defies the mortuary arts.

She lifted a gray and insubstantial arm, slowly, slowly, with one awful finger bone exposed below the sleeve, her black non-eyes compelled him, and her voice moaned above the screeching, "Eat, or be damned! Eat!"

"What?" he whispered. But he knew the answer. He knew too that should that bony finger reach the level of his head, his eyes, its touch would burn like ice, destroying all that was inside his brain, and leaving nothing but the salt-strewn plains of Carthage. Where this wraith touched, no thoughts would ever bloom.

His cheeks were wet with tears of pure terror, and he jibbered, "No! Oh, no! I never meant it. Never would have said... I mean, I only meant to put it in for... Oh, my god...."

But it was much too late for terror or regret, and in the dark his fumbling fingers found his notes beside him, and in dread his tortured mouth began to chew, to eat the very words themselves. The muscles in his misused throat moved of themselves, transporting their ghastly burden, while his salivary glands played their emollient role. His body was attendant to reginal orders from well beyond the tomb.

Nor did the papers on the lectern escape the others' fate, for they were blown, as by the wind across the Styx, and Tony, on his knees like poor, mad Nebuchadnezzar, gathered them up and ate them too, their texture worse than grass, corrasable and clammy on his tongue. Humiliated, on his knees, he then began to choke, but although he was wracked double, retching, nothing re-emerged of all his work, nor would it until it had become in fact that to which the wraith had tacitly compared it.

Poor Tony Lloyd then regained his chair, and now the air was filled with tolling bells, the bells which sobbed the phantom's name, the bells which called across the plains of Petrograd, which fill the fog of Venice, and which sang — who knows? — the fall of Troy: which throw their mournful voices on the wind to celebrate the sacrifice of gods. A loud, insistent peal of bells rang forth, and through it the phantom of the screen, who pointed still at Tony, cried, most horrible of curses, "Scholar, now forget! You will forget! You won't remember, Scholar! Won't remember! Wo-o-on't remember! Woe-oh-oh-on't remember!" Pointing, cursing, damning him to hell, until her voice overcame the bells, and filled the room, and made the walls resound and echo with her words. "You won't remember! Won't remember! Won't!"

The silence was more painful than the din.

It ended in a flash, was gone, went black, and then the lights came up. Anthony Lloyd uncovered his face, and after a moment opened his eyes. His hands lay leaden in his lap, his breath came slowly, fully, and was expelled in gasps, and then was smooth. He stared before him, and took stock, sans slides, sans notes, sans heart, sans — everything. And then he thought, "But I remember. I remember — what? — biography. It's Thursday, and I've written a biography. Of whom? A robber baron, yachted, very rich, who gave his name to – Here! This building all around me. And in an hour or less, I'll give a talk, slides or no: I'll hold them with the brilliance of my insight. And there was something else I had to say, something to hold them, something – what? I can't recall. But it's Thursday, and I have to give my talk."

The men came in the door then and saw two people staring at a blank screen.

Anthony Lloyd, white and shaken, stood up, and turned, and behind him his wife was also standing, prettier than ever, pulling her handbag onto one shoulder, unblinking, as though she had had two martinis.

"Elizabeth," he said, his voice poignant and full of need.

She froze, with her thumb under the strap at her shoulder, and looked at him with clear, bright hazel eyes, smiled slightly, and inclined her head.

"Who are you?" she said.

The bells' curse had found its target.

And now I know you're ready for a drink, and I certainly am.

NOTES ON THE CONTRIBUTORS

HERBERT CAHOON
is the Robert H. Taylor Curator Emeritus of Autograph Manuscripts at the Morgan Library.

INGE DUPONT
is Supervisor of the Reading Room at the Morgan Library.

MARK FARRELL
is Curator of the Robert H. Taylor Collection in the Princeton University Library, where Belle da Costa Greene began her career as a librarian.

JANET ING FREEMAN
formerly Librarian of the Scheide Library, Princeton, now lives in London, within sight of Dibdin's church.

LIRAN LUDELEY
is the pseudonym of an Assistant Curator who worked in the Drawings and Prints Department of the Morgan Library during the tenure of Miss Felice Stampfle. She now lives in Venice and Texas.

RHODA MANSBACH
is a Scottish writer of short stories. She worked in the Cataloguing Department at the Morgan Library for two years and now lives in Iowa.

HOPE MAYO
is Associate Curator of Printed Books at the Morgan Library.

RICHARD PRIEST
was Supervisor of the Reading Room and Acting Curator of Early Printed Books at the Morgan Library.

J. RIGBIE TURNER
is the Mary Flagler Cary Curator of Music Manuscripts and Books at the Morgan Library.

COLOPHON

This book was designed by George Laws and printed by M. A. Gelfand and Jim
Ricciardi. Typefaces are Emerson, for text, and Goudy Bible, for titling. The types
were set and cast at the Out of Sorts Letter Foundry, Mamaroneck, New York.
The wood engravings throughout the book and on the cover are by John De
Pol. Lynn Peterson assisted with proofreading, folding, and collating. The Stone
House Press has provided the reproduction proofs from which
this Fordham University Press edition of 1,000 copies has
been printed on Mohawk Superfine paper.